Cup

and

Curses

POLLY HOLMES

Dear Irene
Enjoy Clair's story
Polly Holmes

Western Australia

COPYRIGHT

Published by Gumnut Press

Copyright © 2019 Polly Holmes

ISBN: 978-0-6485325-2-1

Edited by Nina S. Gooden
(www.greenteaandpinkink.com)

Cover by Mariah Sinclair (www.thecovervault.com)

DEDICATION

For Nina

Your constant support and guidance has been invaluable. My journey as a writer has been an interesting one, and I can honestly say that I would not be where I am today if it wasn't for your words of encouragement when the going gets tough.

Thank you from the bottom of my heart.

ALSO BY POLLY HOLMES

The Cupcake Capers Series

Cupcakes and Cyanide

Cupcakes and Curses

Cupcakes and Corpses

Mistletoe and Murder

Publishers Stocking Polly Holmes Books

Amazon

Gumnut Press

Chapter One

SWEAT BEADED CLAIR McCorrson's forehead as she pulled her aging, red Toyota to an abrupt stop outside the old Sweets mansion. Her gaze caught Mr Hapworth's charcoal-grey BMW, parked across the street. The words *Hapworth Settlement Agents* were branded across the door in bright silver script. Clair could barely contain her excitement.

"I can't believe this beautiful old house is going to be ours in a matter of minutes." It was the perfect location to expand their business and open a new coffee and cupcake shop, CC's Cupcake Haven.

She'd worked her butt off since opening CC's Simply Cupcakes with her sister, Charlotte, three years ago. It was Charlotte who had put them on the map, with her divinely scrumptious award-winning cupcakes while Clair kept the business side under control. Their youngest sister, Cassidy, stayed out of the kitchen and focused on her interior design company. What she loved most about CC's Simply

Cupcakes was eating them. Cassidy's interior design skills had wowed the town folk. Especially, her beautifully designed, vintage-chic-themed interior of the shop.

They were all in agreeance. It was time to branch out. With Charlotte taking charge of the Ashton Point store and Cassidy focused on her interior design company, it freed Clair to make CC's Cupcake Haven her own success story. She even had her bank loan approved and was ready to start renovations as soon as the property settled.

They couldn't believe their luck when the local real estate agent had found this old mansion in a matter of days, and at a very reasonable price, considering the current real estate market in Australia.

"Thank goodness Charlotte loves this house as much as I do," she muttered as she stepped out of the car balancing the box of silver frosted cupcakes in one hand, and her bag and phone in the other. "I hope you have a sweet tooth, Mr Hapworth," Clair said, her mouth still salivating from the aniseed taste tester she'd sampled before leaving the shop. It was

Charlotte's idea to bring a box of cupcakes, specially designed with Mr Hapworth's company logo. As a thank you.

Although Cassidy was away visiting their parents in New York, her tastes mirrored their own. They really couldn't go past the house when they'd found out it was originally owned by a woman named Sweets. According to Charlotte, it was an omen.

It was meant to be.

Clair quickened her step, hopping over a raised paver by the rickety garden gate. She held her breath as the box of treats precariously rocked in her hand, almost tumbling to the ground. "Whoa, that was close. Charlotte would never forgive me if I dropped her master creations." She glanced at her phone and it flashed seven-fifteen. "If there's one thing I hate, it's being late." Her nerves twisted her gut into knots.

Mr Hapworth's words rolled around in her mind. *There's no reason we shouldn't settle on time. Don't you worry about a thing, my dear. I'll take care of everything.*

She hadn't heard from him, so, fingers crossed, everything went through as planned.

As she approached the stained-glass door, she frowned, her gaze searching for Mr Hapworth. They'd agreed to meet on the porch at seven. She bit her bottom lip. Maybe he was waiting inside.

Should I knock or just go straight in? Mum always said never go in uninvited. Her mother had always taught her good manners. She smiled to herself. Even though her parents lived in New York, she still missed them every day, especially her mother. Clair sucked in a lungful of salty air and tapped her knuckles on the glass.

Silence.

The whisper of a warm sea breeze coasting through the nearby trees caught her attention. Clair tapped once more, a little harder this time. The cold sting of the toughened glass was a sharp contrast to the warm summer evening. "Mr Hapworth, are you there? It's Clair McCorrson."

As the wind picked up, the rustle of the trees grew into a dull roar, as if they were coaxing her to enter. *Well, he did say meet him here at seven, and his car is parked out front. He has to be inside.*

Excitement spurred her into action as she turned the rickety, old door handle. The high-pitched creak of the door scraping along the tiles resembled fingernails down a chalkboard.

"Oww," she said, her entire body cringing at the familiar sound. "This door is *definitely* the first thing to get fixed."

She peeked inside and it took a moment for her eyes to adjust to the semi-darkness. The slowly fading, golden rays of sunset streaming through the front windows were enough light to brighten parts of the dull interior. While it was after seven in the evening, they still had daylight saving on the central coast of New South Wales, which meant it was light 'til around nine. A perfect balmy Australian evening.

"Mr Hapworth, are you here?" Clair called from the door. Again, silence met her words. Making her way inside, Clair's gaze scanned the semi-empty house. Her mind raced, excited by the plans she'd already drawn up. She hoped when Cassidy started designing the interior, she'd be able to accentuate its unique charm by keeping most of the old antique furniture left by the previous owner. It would fit perfectly into their vintage-chic branding.

A shiver ran through her spine, as if someone had just walked over her grave.

Something's not right. Where is he? And why hasn't he come out to meet me? The hairs on the back of her neck stood to attention.

Edging herself farther into the house she called once again. "Mr Hapworth, it's Clair McCorrson. I've some yummy cupcake treats here for you." She froze, her words stuck in the back of her throat. All the wind rushed from Clair's lungs in one forceful exhale. Her gaze fell on the limp body of Mr Hapworth, lying twisted at the base of the staircase.

"Mr Hapworth," she said barely above a whisper. The tormented stare of his lifeless eyes glared straight at her. She gasped and her hand shot to her mouth, muffling an impending scream. Clair stared down in disbelief and her hands started to shake as she caught sight of the pool of thick crimson blood beneath his head. There was no question in her mind. James Hapworth was dead.

The blood ran cold in her veins. She'd never seen a real dead body, other than her beautiful Grandma when she'd said good-bye at the funeral. This was different, other end of the scale different. It wasn't at all like in the movies. She stood frozen to the spot for what felt like forever. Clair's mind raced with what to do next, a million thoughts bombarding her all at once. *What do they usually do in the movies? Run.*

Running from your problems never solves anything, her teenage years had taught her that. Clair's gaze caught the edge of a tattered sideboard to the right of the formal lounge room. She managed to place the cupcake box down before dropping it. Dialling the police, her fingers shook so hard she nearly dropped the phone. "Come on, get it together."

In the distance, the creak of the front door was like a clap of thunder rolling in from the sea. She spun, coming face to face with the cold barrel of a gun. Terrified at the prospect of death, her heart skipped a beat.

"Don't move." Robert's stern voice held her frozen to the spot.

"R-Robert?" Clair said with a quiver.

His brow furrowed. "Clair…Clair McCorrson?"

"Yes, Robert, it's me." She glanced down the steely barrel of his gun. "Do you think you could take that gun out of my face? You're scaring the bejesus out of me."

"No can do, I'm afraid. We got an anonymous report that a murder had been committed in this old house." He peered around behind her, absorbing the scene before him. "And by the looks of it, they may have been right." His eerie tone stole her next breath.

Clair's gaze shot to the lifeless body. "You can't possibly think I had anything to do with Mr Hapworth's death."

Robert's eyebrow raised in suspicion. "Mr Hapworth, the settlement agent?"

Clair's jaw dropped. *Oh, my goodness, he does.* Her shaking knees were barely holding her upright. "Um…yes, we were meeting here, only I was running late," Clair's voice rose an octave higher with each word. "I was just about to call you," she said as she held her phone up. "See?"

12

Robert paused, lowering his gun slowly. "Would you mind moving over here, away from the body?"

With pleasure. Her head was pounding so hard she thought it might explode.

Robert holstered his gun. Checking the body for signs of life, he pulled out his radio and called it in. Flicking open his notebook, he cleared his throat and asked, "Can you tell me what happened?"

The shrill of his phone blaring through the silent house was like a flock of galahs at feeding time. He frowned as he noted the number on the screen. "I need to take this."

Clair nodded squeezing her jittery hands together. "Of course."

Robert shuffled her toward the formal lounge room away from the scene of the crime. "Are you okay to wait in here while I take this call? Then we can talk."

"Sure," she said willing his call to be quick. *Seems I don't have much choice.* He parked himself by the front door keeping a watchful eye on her, his voice so quiet she could barely make out a word.

13

"Go ahead, I'm listening…"

I can't believe this is happening. I knew I shouldn't have read my stars today. "Life is going to throw you a curve ball." *Some curveball.* She stood waiting, the distorted image of the body stuck in her mind like mud.

The lingering pungent stench of blood filled her nostrils. Why would anyone want to kill poor Mr Hapworth? She took a moment to think and then the full realisation of her situation finally sunk in.

Holy cow, with the timing of the anonymous tip, they're going to think I murdered him. Means, motive and opportunity, isn't that what they say on *CSI?* She had no motive to kill him, but the other two may appear debatable since she was found alone with his body in an empty house full of potential murder weapons. Is two out of three enough to convict her of murder?

Not if I have anything to say about it.

Robert's voice still babbled away, his attention now diverted toward the body. She only had about forty minutes of daylight left. It was now or never.

Clair ignored the nervous pain in her chest and casually studied the room as if she was admiring the aged decor. If questioned, she could pretend she was planning renovations. She shuddered, goose bumps assaulted her arms. It was as if she could sense the spirit of old Mrs Sweets still there in the room.

Time stood still. A dense layer of dust coated the leftover antique furniture. It looked just as it had on her final inspection, when she had walked through with Mr Hapworth. Her gaze fell on the top of the phone table by the lounge room entrance and she paused.

What the...? A dim ray of sunlight gleamed off the fresh clean circular surface. A perfect circle about the size of a wine bottle base. *It's gone, whatever was there is gone.* Could it have been the murder weapon?

Robert cleared his throat and her body snapped to attention. "Sorry about that. Listen, Clair, it's not my place to judge, but I'm afraid you're going to have to come with me down to the station for further questioning."

"Station? In the back of your police car? But I didn't do anything. I only just arrived about ten minutes before you did. I knocked several times and when there was no answer, I came in and found Mr Hapworth already lying on the ground...dead."

He nodded. "That may be so, but with the anonymous tip we can't leave any stone unturned."

He pocketed his phone. "Now, if you'll come with me, we'll wait in my vehicle until the coroner arrives for the body."

"Wait." Clair paused biting her lip.

"Excuse me?" he asked, with a raised eyebrow.

Should she tell him about the missing object? *The truth always wins* had been the motto in the McCorrson house since she could talk. In this instance, she wasn't so sure. She shook her head. "Nothing."

Robert held the front door open. Clair's feet trudged along the tiled floor as if walking through molasses. She glanced over her shoulder one last time at the phone table, racking her mind over the missing object. Maybe she was jumping to conclusions and there was a simple explanation.

Clair flinched as she headed out of the house and into the backseat of the police car as if she were a common criminal. Thank goodness it wasn't the middle of the day, in broad daylight, for every nosy bystander to see.

She buried her face in her hands. *This can't be happening. It just can't be. I must be in some sort of nightmare. Any minute, I'm going to wake up and see Charlotte's cheeky grin laughing at me, telling me to stop being so silly.*

She owed her sister one big apology. She shouldn't have been so quick to dismiss Charlotte's concerns when she had been in the same predicament not so long ago. Charlotte had mistakenly been accused of spiking her cupcakes with cyanide. The notion seemed absurd, until now.

The flash of red and blue from another oncoming police car jolted her gaze upward. *I wonder if they'll notice the clean spot of the table.* This was clearly a nightmare of the realistic kind.

Having chattered to those who just arrived, Robert pulled away from the curb and headed south toward the station. Her gaze caught his in the rear-view mirror. "How you doing?" he asked.

For a moment she stared at him in blank confusion. *Considering my life has turned into an Agatha Christie movie, I'm doing smashingly.* "How am I doing?" she shrieked. "How do you think I'm doing?"

"No need to get hysterical," Robert said, annoyance clearly evident in his tone. "It's best to stay calm in situations like these."

"Maybe for you, but from where I'm sitting, life looks pretty grim at the moment." Her hands trembled in her lap. "You think I'm a murderer, even though you have no evidence."

"I never said that. I'm just doing my job. You were found standing over a dead body. Procedure dictates that you need to be brought in for questioning and Detective Anderson is eager to speak to you, considering the anonymous caller and all."

She sat back in her seat and folded her arms across her chest, her spirits sinking by the second. "I'd like to tell our precious Detective Anderson exactly what he can do with his procedures."

"I'll pretend I didn't hear that," Robert said under his breath, his eyes focused on the road ahead.

"Pretend all you like, but if you think you're going to pin Mr Hapworth's murder on me, think again." Clair sat in silence for the rest of the way. Her mind meticulously replayed each step of the evening so many times she felt nauseous.

By the time he'd escorted her into an interview room, her jaw was tightly clenched and her body rigid.

The truth always wins.

Anxiousness clawed persistently at the base of her neck. She'd worked hard to build her reputation in this town and she wasn't about to let one little misunderstanding destroy it. Her gaze caught Detective Anderson's stern look as he walked through the door.

"Clair, nice to see you. I wish it were under better circumstances." He pointed to the chair in front of her. "Please have a seat and we'll get this over with as quickly as possible."

"I would appreciate that," she said as she slid into the chair. "This has been a very distressing evening."

"Why don't you start from the beginning," he said, opening his notepad.

She fiddled with the hem of her shirt under the table. Inside she was a simmering bundle of nerves. "There isn't much to tell. We recently purchased the Sweets place for a new cupcake and coffee shop, CC's

Cupcake Haven. I was to meet Mr Hapworth at the house at seven to receive the final settlement documents. I was running late and got there at about seven-fifteen. His car was parked across the street, so I knew he was there, but he wasn't on the porch which is where we agreed to meet. I assumed he was waiting inside, I just didn't know he'd be dead. I swear." She took a gulp of the chilled water at the end of the table easing the scratchy dryness of her throat.

"Go on."

"I knocked on the door and there was no answer. Then I called out, still no answer. The door was unlocked, so I went in and then I called for Mr Hapworth again. Still no answer and that's when I spotted him lying on the floor…he wasn't moving and there was so much blood. I knew he was dead." She squeezed her eyes shut a moment. Remembering the beautiful way her Grandma looked at her wake is the way a person should leave this world. Old age, not murder.

"Clair, are you all right? Do you need a break?" he asked, his voice full of compassion.

Her eyelids flew open. "No. I'm fine. I just want to get this over with so I can go home."

He nodded and continued. "Whose idea was it to meet at the house?"

She paused and shivered, the air suddenly feeling like a frosty winters morning. "Mine."

His eyebrow raised and he scribbled unreadable notes as she spoke. "Why meet so late at night?" he asked. "I know it's daylight saving, but surely, you were worried about being there in the dark. After all, there's been no electricity since Mrs Sweets passed on."

"I know, but I figured it would be a great idea to finalise all the details where my next adventure was about to start. You know, take a picture out front so I could hang it inside when the shop opens. Seven was the only time Mr Hapworth could do it and since it's still daylight saving, it doesn't get completely dark 'til around nine, so there'd be plenty of light. It wasn't like it was going to be a long meeting, I hadn't even intended on going inside. Grab the docs, take a picture…" She slapped her forehead and gasped. "The cupcakes."

"Cupcakes?"

"Yes, I left the cupcakes at the house. Charlotte made aniseed cupcakes for Mr Hapworth, complete with his silver logo. I know there were other people interested in the property. They were a kind of thank you for helping me secure the property and I left them there on the sideboard in the foyer."

"I wouldn't be too worried about the cupcakes, unless Charlotte decided to start cooking with cyanide this time." His smug tone taunted Clair. "Please continue."

"As I said, I was there to close the deal. That's it. Murder wasn't exactly at the top of my to-do list."

"So, there was nothing unusual in the house when you entered?"

She shook her head. "No, like I said, it was so still…cold almost."

"Did you see anyone near the house, in a car perhaps or driving away, as you arrived?" he asked.

"There were a few cars coming and going, none that I knew, but I didn't really take much notice. I was there for one reason only." Frustration was slowly bleeding through her limbs.

He shoved an evidence bag across the table. "Are these the documents you were to receive?"

Clair's attentive gaze scanned the front page. A smear of blood obscured half the words. "Yes. They're mine. What happens to them now?" she asked more abruptly than she'd meant to.

"They're evidence for the time being," he said as he continued to write.

"Evidence? But you can't hold them. I'm really sorry about Mr Hapworth, but he was going to confirm everything went through on time when we spoke this evening. What am I supposed to do now? It's not like he has a partner I can turn to."

"You'll have to wait until this mess is sorted and Mr Hapworth's killer is brought to justice."

He can't be serious.

Clair already had her first loan repayment due in a month, she'd go broke if she didn't get the coffee shop up and running soon.

"If I were you, instead of worrying about starting your next adventure, I'd be worrying about going to jail for murder."

Murder? Clair felt the blood drain from her face. *I didn't kill anyone.* "Mark my words, Detective Anderson, I will not be going to jail for any murder. I am innocent."

He stood and closed his notepad. "Let me give you the same advice I gave your sister, Charlotte, not so long ago. Don't go getting yourself into trouble or into a situation that will put you in danger. Leave the investigating to the professionals."

Clair stood eye to eye with Detective Anderson, anger smouldering through her veins like a potent drug. "Yes. And look how that turned out. If I remember rightly, Charlotte solved the mystery of the cyanide poisonings. Wrapped it up in a nice little bundle for you. If it weren't for her investigation—"

"I think the correct word is 'snooping,' and she was lucky we arrived when we did or it could have turned out completely different," he barked, snatching the evidence bag off the table.

"Call it what you will, but if it weren't for Charlotte doing *your* job for you, she could have been the one in jail for murder, instead of the rightful killer who almost succeeded in framing her."

His lips thinned and Clair could see his cheeks begin to redden. "Still, leave the investigating to the police. Don't leave town and if we need to question you further, we'll be in touch. I'll have Robert take you home."

"Fine. But if I'm under suspicion of murder, I'd appreciate being kept in the loop since it is my future hanging in the balance."

"I'm sure we'll be in touch," he said holding the door open. "As for keeping you in the loop, we don't normally tell persons of interest what we've found until we're ready to make an arrest."

"Persons of interest? We'll see about that," she said as she stormed out of the interview room, flicking her bouncy red curls over her shoulder as she left.

Chapter Two

CLAIR TOSSED RESTLESSLY. Her closed eyelids fluttered as she slept, the events of last night running through her head.

"Prisoner Clair McCorrson you have been charged with murder, how do you plead?"

"Not guilty, your honour," Clair yelled from the witness box, silent tears streaming down her cheeks.

Hysterical fits of laughter burst from the viewing gallery. She turned and spotted her family at the back of the courtroom. But they weren't her family anymore. They were menacing clowns, laughing, yelling vulgar accusations at her.

"No, no, no," she pleaded with them. "I didn't murder him. Stop it. Stop laughing at me."

That only made them laugh harder and chant her name. She couldn't breathe. Couldn't process the nightmare unfolding before her.

A giggling lime-green clown hosting a bright-pink, frizzy hairdo shot up like a firecracker from her seat and yelled obscenities at her, chanting her name like the roar of an angry lion. The voice sounded like Charlotte,   but   it   couldn't   be. *"Clair...Clair...Clair...Clair..."*

Clair's eyes flew open and she bolted upright in her bed, gasping for air, Charlotte's voice ringing in her head. Her pulse was racing its own hundred-meter sprint in world-record time. She sucked in mouthfuls of air.

"Clair, are you all right? Calm down and breathe slowly," said Charlotte in a panicked tone. "Take some deep breaths."

Clair squeezed her eyes shut, the pain in her chest subsiding as her breathing slowly returned to a comfortable rhythm. "Holy cow." Thank Goodness it was just a nightmare and not reality. *Yet.*

Charlotte flopped down and stretched out along the foot of the bed. "I've been calling your name for ages. Must have been a doozy of a nightmare. Don't suppose it had anything to do with this?" Charlotte asked as she held up the front page of the morning newspaper.

Clair's jaw dropped and her eyes widened. "What the… Cupcake Killer strikes again?" Her lips thinned and she sucked in air through her nose. Clair's hand flew to her chest, the stabbing pain returning ten-fold. "I am not a killer, much less a cupcake killer."

Charlotte's eyebrows raised. "Forget to tell me something last night, huh?"

She snatched the paper out of Charlotte's hands, her eyes eagerly reading each sentence in depth. Her head began to pound under the weight of the printed accusations.

"Police caught Clair McCorrson standing over the dead body of local settlement agent, James Hapworth, yesterday evening." *I don't believe what I'm reading.* "A secret meeting in an abandoned house, pre-arranged by Ms McCorrson. History has it, the rickety old Mansion is cursed. Has the spirit of Mrs Sweets returned to haunt the people of Ashton Point? One red-head in particular? Is Clair as innocent as she claims, or did she maliciously plan the perfect murder?"

Cursed…the perfect murder? Is there a sign on our shop that says, 'blame every murder in Ashton Point on the McCorrson sisters?'

"Hey, I don't mean to be rude, but I do think you have some explaining to do. Did you know the building was cursed before you put the offer in on it?" Charlotte asked as she pushed up to a sitting position.

Clair threw her doona back over Charlotte and grabbed her dressing gown. "Don't be ridiculous, there is no such thing as curses. They don't exist. This is way too much for my head before coffee," she said, storming toward the kitchen, Charlotte hot on her heels.

"Life's always fun and games for the McCorrson sisters," Charlotte said jokingly.

Clair spun, glaring at her sister. "This is no joking matter." She shook the paper in front of Charlotte's amused expression. "They're saying I murdered Mr Hapworth."

"Okay, I'm sorry," Charlotte said, holding her hands up in defence.

Coffee. Everything always seems better after coffee, she thought, continuing her journey to the kitchen.

"But how is this any different from when they accused me of putting cyanide in my cupcakes at Beth's wedding and then plastered it all over the front page?" Charlotte crossed her arms and waited patiently.

Clair closed her eyes, pressing her fingers to her temples. *Coffee. I need caffeine.* "Please, Charlotte, can you at least wait until I've had my coffee? I didn't exactly sleep well last night," she pleaded.

"Sure. You may as well make me one while you're at it."

Clair busied herself at the kitchen bench, her body tense. *Where on earth did they get the information from? And why would they print my name in the paper, when there is no concrete evidence?* News travels fast in a small town, but this had to take the cake.

She breathed a sigh of relief as the frothy hazelnut liquid slid down her throat and warmed her from the inside out. Her fizzled brain was starting to think normally again. "I'm sorry," Clair said.

Charlotte's brow creased.

Clair continued, swallowing a cup of humility as she spoke. "I'm sorry for snapping just now and I'm sorry I was so blasé when you were freaking out over the accusations against you."

"Thanks, I appreciate that." Charlotte smiled warmly.

"On the positive, you did score a boyfriend out of the fiasco."

Charlotte's cheeks blossomed a rosy red. "I know, lucky me. Who knew Ashton Point's wedding of the year could have been so disastrous and wonderful at the same time?" Clair couldn't help but smile at her sister's happiness. It had been Lincoln's best man, Liam, who'd helped Charlotte clear her name, stealing her heart in the process.

Clair re-read the entire article from top to bottom, scrutinizing every word. She'd heard rumours about a curse but never taken much notice of it. Now she wished she had. "It pretty much says here in black and white that I murdered Mr Hapworth."

"I guess, but people will know that it's total garbage."

"Will they?" Clair asked. "How are they going to know? It basically says that I planned the whole thing. Arranged the meeting late at night and deliberately had it at the mansion. It even says I was affected by some sort of curse. Either way, it makes me look guilty." She paused taking a deep breath.

Her gaze fell on the journalist's name. "What I don't get is how Christina Jacobs knows so much about the events of last night. I mean, by the time I got back home from the police station it was after eleven. And it wasn't like it was full of people. As far as I was aware, only Robert and Detective Anderson were on duty. Even Alison at the front desk had gone home."

Charlotte pursed her lips. "I suppose she has her sneaky journalist ways of finding things out, and since she's owned *The Chronicle* for over ten years, she probably knows a lot more about this town than we gave her credit for. She probably has secret contacts hiding in the most unusual places. Maybe we should have asked her about the Sweets mansion before making an offer."

Clair shook her head. "Still, I'm going to find out how she found out this information so quickly. I can't see Robert or Detective Anderson blabbing to her." It was hard to control the frustration that mounted with every breath she took.

"This could get really ugly if it's not handled properly," Charlotte said. "The cyanide debacle was bad enough, now this. The business can only take so much before people start losing faith in us and we've worked too hard to let that happen."

Clair clenched her fingers into tight fists as Charlotte's words registered. *Not to mention finding some extra money to make the first loan repayment.* "I promise I will not let that happen. I did not do this horrible thing and if I have to prove it, I will. The sooner I get it sorted the better."

"You have my vote of support," Charlotte said in a hyped tone.

Clair leant against the stone kitchen bench, looking at Charlotte, her brows creased in thought. She couldn't help mulling over the missing object from the phone table.

"Is something wrong?" Charlotte asked.

"I'm not sure. When you did the final walk through of the house with me, did you notice what was on the phone table by the entrance to the formal lounge room?"

"I can't say I did, I was in heaven admiring the commercial-sized kitchen. Why do you ask?"

"Well, last night while I was waiting for Robert to finish his phone call, I noticed there was a clean circle, void of dust. It was obvious something was missing."

Charlotte's eyes widened and her jaw dropped. "You don't suppose it was the murder weapon?"

Clair nodded, but before she could answer, the buzz of the doorbell interrupted their conversation.

"What now?" Clair asked, throwing her hands up in the air, her eye catching the newspaper headline one more time. *Please don't be a nosy local, wanting more gossip, or worse, the local media.*

Charlotte stood. "Want me to get it?"

Annoyance tightened Clair's jaw. "No, I'll get it. Can't have people think I'm hiding behind my little sister when the going gets tough."

Clair's hand stilled on the door handle. Nervous knots welled in the pit of her stomach. *Please don't let me make a fool of myself.*

Rolling her shoulders back, she opened the door. "Can I…" She froze when the man before her turned. Her words caught in the back of her throat.

If he's the press, he can interview me any day.

She stood staring into the most gorgeous, deep, Mediterranean-blue eyes, masked only by a pair of thick, black-rimmed glasses. His hair had just the right amount of messy for it to look like a model's.

He pushed his glasses up on his nose. "Clair McCorrson?"

Butterflies overtook her nerves. "Yes."

He looked her up and down. Goose bumps assaulted every inch of her body under his heavy scrutiny. "I was wondering if I could ask you some questions about James Hapworth?" His soft tone almost threw her, but Clair mentally cautioned herself.

Don't be fooled by his good looks and debonair voice. "I'm sorry, you've caught me at a bad time and I'm not really up for giving an interview."

His eyebrows went up in question. "Excuse me?"

With her focus regained, she folded her arms across her chest. Power and strength soared through her body. "I'm sorry, regardless of what's printed in that silly paper. I'm extremely busy and I'm sure you'll be able to source your information elsewhere."

"I think you've got the wrong idea," he said, his words full of sincerity.

"Really? So, you haven't come to ask me what happened last night at the Sweets mansion?"

He shuffled on the spot and his nervous movements put her on edge. "Yes, I have, but I'm not from the media if that's what you think." He ran his hand through his dishevelled hair. "My name is Mason... Mason Hapworth. James Hapworth is...was my father."

Clair's jaw dropped and her blood turned to ice. *Mason Hapworth?* Clair tensed and pulled her gown tighter. "Oh." She'd heard James had a son, but they didn't exactly get on. Apparently, they hadn't been able to stand the sight of each other and he'd left Ashton Point some years ago. At least, that's what she'd heard on the town grapevine. Whenever she mentioned family, he'd always been hush-hush about his. "I'm very sorry for your loss."

"Thank you. The police informed me of my father's death last night and I thought it only right to come and see for myself the woman they say is a person of interest in his murder," he said, his gaze never leaving Clair's.

"But it's not true. I didn't murder your father. It was all a terrible mistake." Her hands grew clammy and she tried to keep her breath measured but she failed miserably. "Everything they printed was a lie."

His brow creased. "Printed? I have no idea what you're talking about. I drove down last night from Surfers Paradise and spoke to a Detective Anderson at the police station this morning."

"Oh. I suppose he told you that it was all me, thanks to that stupid curse garbage. I'm sure that by now everyone in town is convinced I did it as well."

"I'm not sure what curse you're talking about. He informed me that he still hasn't received the results of the autopsy, but they were questioning someone in relation to the incident. He refused to tell me any more information." He paused and there was no mistaking the determination in his voice. "I know it's been almost ten years since I've lived here, but it seems not much has changed. Once the gossip train gets hold of a story, it never lets it go."

"It didn't take long to find out who Detective Anderson was referring to. So, here I am to ask you face to face." He took a step closer, his ocean-blue eyes holding her in a trance. "Did you have anything to do with my father's death?"

It felt like forever before she spoke. "No, no, no. I had absolutely nothing to do with your father's death, I swear." *Will he believe me?* "I can explain everything."

"Explain?" he asked with a raised eyebrow. "You were found alone, in an empty house standing over his bloodied body."

"Yes, I was but…"

He stood there, his eyes drilling hers. "But what? What is there that you can explain that the police won't be able to uncover in their investigation?"

"It really is all a simple misunderstanding." She smiled, hoping to ease the growing tension. "A simple misunderstanding of wrong place, wrong time."

He paused and his brow creased. "My father wasn't the easiest person to get along with. I know he had enemies, but you don't strike me as one."

"I'm not. He was my settlement agent, that's all. I swear."

"You don't look like someone who would take another's life. Then again, I don't know you," he said hoarsely, then spun and walked away.

Clair froze as she watched his retreating figure. She rattled off the first word that popped into her mind. "Coffee."

He stopped and turned at the high-pitch sound of her voice. "Excuse me?"

Clair's voice shook. "You could get to know me and then you'll have no reason to ever think I could do something as horrific as murder. I promise I won't take up too much of your time and you did say you'd been traveling. If you're anything like me when I travel, you must be in desperate need of caffeine. The good stuff." She bit her bottom lip as she waited for his answer. One more supporter on her side couldn't hurt.

His brow furrowed as if he were tossing her proposition around in his mind.

The corner of his lips turned up into a sheepish grin. "You're right about one thing, I am in need of a good coffee. I guess I could hear your side of the story."

She stepped back to hold the door open. "Please come in and I'll explain everything over a hazelnut Nespresso."

Mason smiled and advanced toward her, his muscular frame filling the doorway. He paused, his eyes pinning her back up against the wall. "Thank you, Clair."

Clair sucked in a deep breath. The spicy scent of his aftershave caught her off guard. She shook her head. *Far out, woman. Surely it hasn't been that long since you've had a boyfriend.* It dawned on her just how pathetic her love life really was. No wonder she was salivating over a perfect stranger. A stranger who had just lost his father no less. *How callous can I be?*

He paused and his gaze turned on her. "If you'd rather, we can always have coffee downtown at Tea 4 Two Café?"

Like I want more inquisitive, nosy people staring at me. Would they be staring because of the rumours or because they were wondering what a woman like me is doing out in public with a guy like you?

"No imposition at all." She smiled. "I was just thinking what a shock it must have been when Detective Anderson called to tell you about your father."

"Yes, you could say that."

She closed the door and moved past him, holding her breath as she went. "Follow me, it's this way to the kitchen." He moved silently behind like a stealth cat marking his prey. Thank goodness Charlotte had made herself scarce. Clair cringed at the thought of explaining why she let a strange man into their house.

"Nice house," he said, his words slicing the tense air. "Is it yours?"

Clair showed him where to sit while she busied herself with the coffee machine. She shook her head.

"No, my parents. We moved here about three years ago to be close to my grandma. She was a very independent woman and after her second husband passed, she refused to leave her home just because she was getting old, so we came to her."

"What was her name? Maybe I knew her," Mason said fiddling with the salt and pepper shaker on the kitchen table.

"Betty, Betty Brookson," Clair said as she placed a steaming coffee in front of him.

A warm smile spread across his face. "B1 and B2," he said under his breath.

"Excuse me?" Horrified that her grandmother would be referred to as a character from a children's television show. "You did not just compare my beautiful Grandmother to the Bananas-in-Pyjamas, did you?"

"My apologies. I didn't mean to upset you. I do remember her. She was the sweetest, kindest woman. I remember how happy she was married to Bob. They were inseparable. *They* coined the term B1 and B2. They were never apart. They even finished each other's sentences."

Clair shoved her hands on her hips, racking her brain for one instance when she'd heard her grandmother referred to as a banana. "Then how come I haven't heard that term before? I've been living here for three years and no-one else has referred to them as B1 and B2."

He shrugged. "Don't know why. Maybe it was too long ago and people have forgotten, or once Bob passed, it wasn't appropriate anymore." He paused, a frown marring his expression. "I was sorry to hear about her passing last year."

Clair's chest suddenly felt like it was being squashed in a vice. Tears burned like acid in her eyes. The memory of her grandmother's funeral was as sharp today as it had been twelve months ago. "Thank you. That's very kind. I do miss her terribly. I can't imagine what you must be going through. I lost my grandmother to old age. At least I got a chance to say goodbye, but losing your father the way you did must be just awful." His face drained of colour and she could have kicked herself for being so insensitive.

"You can never really prepare yourself." He paused and cleared his throat. "If you're ready, I'd like you to tell me exactly what happened last night. And please, don't leave anything out."

Her tight chest was suddenly replaced by the growing lump in her throat. She licked her lips and dove head first into the same explanation she'd told Detective Anderson last night, barely taking a breath between sentences. By the time she finished her story, her head was pounding.

She sighed. "So, you see I was just in the wrong place at the wrong time. And this silly article." Clair paused and slid the paper across the table. Her words continued to flow like a gushing creek while Mason read. "It practically says I'm a murderer which is just not true. Sure, it was my idea to meet at the house, but he chose the time. I did not have anything to do with your father's death. I'm sure *The Chronicle* just enjoys printing false accusations about people."

Anticipation bubbled inside Clair's gut as he seemed to mull over her words, his eyes glued to the front page. *Why didn't he visit his father?* "I hope you

44

don't mind me asking, but why haven't I ever seen you around town?"

He continued to read as he spoke, his voice emotionless. "My father and I didn't exactly get on. I suppose it was easier to live separate lives. We were never close, less so after my mother passed. In fact, I couldn't wait to move out as soon as I was old enough and could support myself. I've probably returned five or six times at the most, in the last ten years. Life was easier to communicate by email or phone."

"Oh."

A twinge of regret bellowed in the base of her chest. She'd been so focused on her own dramas the last time her parents visited, she'd practically ignored them. A situation she promised to remedy the next time they were in town. Her chest knotted just thinking about losing one of her parents. *Maybe he could do with something stronger than coffee.*

"From what you've told me, at this point, I'm not sure there is enough evidence to indicate that you had anything to do with my father's death. Other than being as you say, 'in the wrong place at the wrong time.'"

"I couldn't agree with you more." Clair sighed with relief.

"I guess I'll wait 'til the police have finished their investigation to make my final conclusions."

"Not me," Clair said shaking her head. "I intend to prove to everyone that I am an innocent victim in this tragedy."

"What exactly do you mean?" he asked, concern etched in his brow.

She stood and placed his empty coffee cup into the dishwasher. "Exactly what I said. I intend to find the culprit, before I end up wearing prison greens 'til I'm old, grey and wrinkly."

Mason stood as if to protest, his chair scraping on the tiles. His words were interrupted by a rapid pounding thump on the front door. Charlotte appeared from the hallway, sliding her arms into a turquoise cotton pullover. "What on earth is that racket?" She paused, eyebrows raised, her gaze shooting from Clair to Mason then back again. "Oops, sorry, I didn't realise you had company."

"It's like Grand Central Station around here this morning. Charlotte, this is Mason Hapworth, James Hapworth's son. Mason, this is my younger sister, Charlotte." The increasing racket at the front door was worse than kid's day at the Royal Show. "If you'll excuse me a moment," Clair said.

She opened the door and paused. Detective Anderson stood on the other side, doing his best Sherlock Holmes impersonation. Robert was standing one step behind him and cleared his throat, shoving his notebook back in his trouser pocket. Judging by the looks on their faces, it wasn't a social visit. Clair could almost hear her heart beating inside her ribcage as they stood there in silence waiting for her to speak. She nodded at each man. "Detective Anderson...Robert."

"Morning, Clair. May we come in?" he asked.

"Of course. I'm not sure the reason for your visit, but I can't tell you any more than I did last night," she said, her anxiety growing by the second.

He pushed past her and headed toward the kitchen, stopping short when his gaze fell on Mason. "Mr Hapworth, I didn't expect to see you here."

"I'm sure you didn't," Mason said, his tone serious.

"Why the house call, Detective?" Charlotte asked, edging closer to Clair.

"I wish we were here under more pleasant circumstances," he said. His words doubled the tension in the room. "Clair, do you know a man by the name of Roland Trent?"

Roland Trent? "The name sounds familiar, but I can't say I do." She turned to Charlotte. "Have you heard of him before?"

Charlotte paused. Clair could almost see the cogwheels clicking over in her mind. "Wasn't he that businessman that moved into the Sampson Office Building in Watson's Creek a month or so ago? I'm sure he was involved in the new property development Mr Hutson was working on before his untimely death."

She frowned, turning her gaze back to Detective Anderson. "Yes, I think you're right. Although I've never met him."

"Where were you, between the hours of one and three this morning?"

Where most normal people are. "Fast asleep. Why do you ask?"

"Can anyone vouch for you?" His words were like a double-edged sword, stabbing her in the heart. *I wish.* "Unfortunately, no."

"Roland Trent's body was found behind the dumpster at the back of CC's Simply Cupcakes in the early hours of this morning. Murdered."

"Murdered!" The girls said in unison.

Clair's voice shot up an octave or two. "Are you for real?"

"Afraid so. We'd appreciate it if you would accompany us to the station for further questioning," he said. "I have a few loose ends that need clearing up."

"Detective, what other evidence do you have that ties Clair to this man's death?" Mason asked as he stepped forward shielding Clair.

"As I just said, at the moment we're just following up with some questions." The skin grew taut across Anderson's jaw.

Charlotte stepped up beside Mason, folding her arms across her chest. Clair swallowed the lump in her throat at the look of determination in her expression. "You're going to need to do better than that."

Clair's stomach began to roll with frustration at the irritated look of Anderson's face. *This is crazy* since she was innocent, surely the evidence would exonerate her.

"If necessary, I'm sure we can get an arrest warrant," Detective Anderson said glaring at Charlotte.

A soft breath eased from Clair's tight lips and she stepped forward, brand new knots forming in her gut and making her head whirl. "That won't be necessary, Detective. It's quite all right," she said, placing her hand on Charlotte's forearm. "I didn't have anything to do with either death, so I have nothing to hide. I'm happy to accompany you to the station."

"Clair—"

Clair shook her head. "No, Charlotte. This nightmare has gone on long enough. The sooner it is sorted, the better."

She turned to Mason and smiled. "Thank you for the vote of confidence."

His smile was like a ray of sunshine breaking through the darkened storm clouds. "Don't worry, Charlotte and I won't be far behind you," Mason said pulling his car keys from his pocket, his gaze sending a firm message to both policemen; don't mess with me.

Chapter Three

"WHAT'S TAKING THEM so long? Feels like she's been in there for hours," Mason said as he paced the foyer of the police station, his nerves as highly strung as a tightrope walker.

Charlotte huffed. "It's hardly been hours." She glanced at the wall clock. "But you're right, she has been in there for a while. I can't possibly imagine why they need to speak to her for so long."

First, the news of his father death, then this Roland guy and now Clair was facing goodness knows what. Even though they'd only just met, he didn't get a sense she was capable of such an atrocity. If anything, he thought the opposite.

Mason took the seat next to Charlotte and dropped his head in his hands. *Oh, Dad. What have you gotten yourself involved in?* He sat, the events of the last twenty-four hours jumbled in his mind like an out-of-order jig-saw puzzle. Charlotte's voice broke through his stupor.

"I'm really sorry to hear about your father."

He eased back in the chair, resting his head against the wall. "Thank you. We weren't close. My life and his didn't really mesh, but I never wanted him dead." Even though there was no love lost between him and his father, he was Mason's flesh and blood and he hadn't deserved to be murdered.

"Of course not," Charlotte said horrified. "I just hope they find the real killer."

He shot from his seat as if bitten on the backside by a bull ant, unable to sit still a moment longer. Worry pumped through his veins. "Listen, I'm going to take a walk to the café next door, grab a coffee and clear my head for a few minutes. Do you want one?"

She smiled and nodded. "Sure. Skim milk latte."

He acknowledged her request with a nod and exited the police station.

Mason gazed up and down the street as he stood by the counter, waiting for his order. It seemed that word of his return had made its way around town. An odd, but familiar sensation scurried through his body as inquisitive gazes started turning in his direction. Mason couldn't really blame them. He'd only been back to Ashton Point a handful of times and most people in town knew he was estranged from his father. It had been that way for the past ten years, since Mason's seventeenth birthday

A sweet innocent voice startled him from behind. "Mason? Mason Hapworth?"

His head whipped around and he paused as Mrs Stevenson's smile lit up the sidewalk. "Why, it is you. I'd know those baby blues anywhere."

He smiled. "Hi, Mrs Stevenson. It's been a while. You're looking amazing, and young as ever."

A shy, crimson blush worked its way across her face. "Oh, stop it. You always were a charmer." Her eyes suddenly softened and she clasped his hands in hers. "I'm very sorry to hear about your father. I know you didn't have the best relationship, but I know he loved you very much."

Loved? I guess he did, in his own odd way. His love for his family paled in insignificance when it came to the next big real estate sale. James Hapworth's version of family love was best received from afar.

"Are you back in town for long, dear?" she asked.

"Only as long as it takes to sort out my father's affairs."

A frown added more wrinkles to her forehead. "I don't often get mad, but when I read that nonsense in the paper this morning, I almost fell off my rocking chair. That Christina Jacobs has a lot to say for herself. How dare she think poor Clair had anything to do with James' death. The McCorrson sisters are the sweetest girls in town and they make the most amazing cupcakes. I swear, I've put on ten pounds, just thinking about those sweet gems. Have you met them yet?"

Mason rocked from one foot to the other, an uncomfortable sensation settling in his chest. "So, you haven't heard?"

She frowned adding another few wrinkles to her tired forehead. "Heard what dear?"

Wow, something he knew that the Ashton Point gossip vine didn't. "They found the body of

Roland Trent behind CC's Simply Cupcakes in the early hours of this morning. He'd been murdered. They have Clair in for questioning as we speak, in relation to both murders." The taste of bile rose in the back of his throat. He cringed at mentioning Clair and murder in the same sentence.

She gasped and her hand flew to her chest as if he'd pierced it with a bullet. "That is the most outrageous piece of information I've ever heard and believe me, I've heard some doozies in my time. Why, just the other day, I saw that Roland man in a heated discussion with Stella Roseamund down from the Classic Curl and I don't think he was a very happy chap."

Roland Trent and Stella Roseamund? The last time he'd spoken to his father, he and Stella had been an item. Granted, that had been some time ago.

A petite woman yelled from behind the coffee machine. "Coffee order for Mason."

Turning, he grabbed the tray of coffees from the counter. "If you'll excuse me, Mrs Stevenson, I really should head back." Mason froze as she clutched his shoulder.

"That poor woman couldn't hurt a fly. Promise me you'll help Clair? Promise me you won't let her go to jail," she said, his shoulder numbing under her tense grip. "In my opinion, neither man was a saint so there is probably a list of people a mile long who had it in for them."

"Thanks for the heads up. I'm not sure what I can do, but yes, I'll do my best to help her any way I can." He held tight as she gave him a motherly hug.

"Take care, dear," she said, waving over her shoulder as she left.

"I can assure you, the truth will come out eventually," Clair said as she marched out of the interrogation room. *Even if I have to find the answers myself.* Anger simmered like a bubbling cauldron deep in her belly. "How dare he tell me not to get upset?"

Detective Anderson was quick to point the finger, but when she countered his argument, he cut her down as quick as a roast lamb on Christmas day.

She paused at the door of the foyer, her hand frozen on the chilled door handle. *He's still here.* Heat warmed her cheeks as the concern deep in his gaze hit her square in the chest. Why couldn't she have met him without the murder charges hanging over her head?

Charlotte shot up from her chair and tore off toward Alison, who was sitting behind the counter, her lips pressed together.

Oh no, this doesn't look good. Clair pushed through the door, catching Charlotte's eye as she moved.

"Oh, thank goodness," Charlotte said, throwing her arms around Clair's neck, almost bowling her over. "About time, are you all right?"

Clair moulded into her sister's loving embrace. The strawberry scent of her hair assaulted Clair's nostrils, while Mason's deep, piercing gaze melted her knees where she stood. Pulling back, she smiled at them both. "I'm fine, really. I'm just so frustrated that anyone would think I could do that to another human being."

"I don't." The deep timbre of Mason's voice bled through her veins like lava.

"Neither do I. What happened in there?" Charlotte asked.

"Um…" she paused, her gaze caught Mason's as he stepped closer.

With an upward twist of his lips, he said. "I'm guessing it was mostly about my father. Am I right?"

Clair nodded.

"If you're worried that talking about him will somehow make me feel uncomfortable, don't be. Even though we weren't close, I do want to find out who did this to him. Maybe it will help me understand him a bit better. I'm as eager as Charlotte to hear what happened."

"Are you sure?" she asked.

"I wouldn't have said it if I wasn't." He slid his glasses up his nose.

The deep, throaty voice of Adele blared from Charlotte's back pocket, rocking through the station foyer. She blushed, checking the screen. "It's Suzi," she mouthed. "Hi, Suzi, what's up?"

Confusion crossed Mason's expression and Clair whispered. "Suzi works for us at CC's Simply Cupcakes. She runs the front counter, which frees up

Charlotte to design, while Pierre helps out with the baking on a part-time basis." His mouth rounded in an O.

"Are you serious? They can't do that, who do they think they are?" Charlotte snapped.

Clair mentally crossed her fingers and prayed there wasn't another murder.

"No, that's okay. You go pick up your mother from the doctors and we'll let you know what happens. We're on our way. Bye." Charlotte shoved the phone back in her pocket. Her murderous glare would rival the best supervillain's. "You'll never believe this, but Robert just turned up at the shop with a search warrant. Apparently, they have cause to search CC's Simply Cupcakes for the murder weapon."

Clair fumed, the breath tightening in her chest. "Seriously? Anderson works fast I'll give him that. He said they were going to be looking further into my affairs, but I didn't think he meant CC's Simply Cupcakes." Her innocent words had obviously fallen on deaf ears. Eyeing the exit, she turned and headed out. "Come on, which way is the car?"

"It's out the back of the station, parked next to mine," Mason said pushing past her to the exit. He held the door open for them. "Would you mind if I tagged along?"

"Not at all," Charlotte said before Clair could say a word.

"Maybe you could tell us what happened after you sort out this debacle with Robert at the shop."

"Sure," Clair said. She let her eyes wander over the plain, black, button-up shirt he wore and noticed uncomfortably that it accentuated his broad shoulders. The shirt made her wonder what was under the rest of his clothing. Her gaze caught his Mediterranean-blue eyes, even they melted her heart just a little. *Oh, my goodness, I'm facing a murder charge and all I can do is ogle the victim's son.*

"Wonderful," Charlotte said as she linked her arm through Clair's and guided her down the front stairs.

Clair stared at Charlotte's sudden enthusiasm. "What is with you?"

Charlotte smiled at Mason over her shoulder as he followed behind, then turned to Clair with a mischievous gleam in her eye. "You can't tell me you're not happy that he's coming along. He's not that hard on the eyes. In fact, some would say he's kind of cute, in a Clark Kent, Superman way."

"That's the problem," Clair whispered. "He's too cute and I should be focusing on the person trying to frame me for murder, not looking for a boyfriend."

"Who said anything about boyfriend?" Charlotte's voice trailed off as they approached her car. "Mason, stay close and you can follow us to the shop."

"No problem," he said.

As Charlotte pulled up outside CC's Simply Cupcakes, Clair saw the commotion outside the shop and she cringed. Mason pulled up behind the police car, two doors down from the shop. "Great, looks like everyone within a country mile is out to see what all the fuss is about."

The girls were on the warpath gunning for the policeman straight ahead, Mason joining behind them. "What is the meaning of this, Robert?" Clair demanded.

He held up a piece of paper. "It's all here in the search warrant."

Charlotte snatched the warrant and read it from top to bottom. "It says here you're looking for a solid, round object?"

Like the missing object from the phone table.

"Yes, that's right." He held his arm out and directed them away from the gathering crowd. "Listen, I'm sure Anderson is just trying to rule you out as a suspect."

Clair saw red and felt her world crumbling around her ears. "Or convict me of murder. How long do you expect this to take?"

Robert shrugged. "Could take an hour, could take all day."

"All day?" Clair shrieked. "But…"

Mason edged in behind her and placed his warm hand on her shoulder. His softened touch seemed to calm her. "Maybe we should let them do their jobs. After all, I'm sure we can occupy ourselves in other ways."

"Listen to your friend. If you'll excuse me, I need to get back to the search," Robert said as he walked away.

Clair felt heat work its way up her neck and settle in her cheeks. Her wide eyes stared at him and in record time he blushed, suddenly aware of the words he spoke.

Charlotte quickly dragged Clair toward the corner. Mason joined them, forming a huddle to isolate Clair away from prying ears. "Clair, what happened back at the police station?" Charlotte asked.

Clair gulped back the lump in her throat. Butterflies began a ramped march inside her stomach and it had nothing to do with what she was about to say and everything to do with the gorgeous man standing within arms-reach. "Here, you want me to tell you here?"

"Yes, the sooner the better. Why were you in with Detective Anderson for so long?"

Before she answered, Clair made sure there was no-one close enough to hear. "After we got through the typical mundane questions, I was finally able to get some concrete information out of him. You're never going to believe this, but both men were killed the exact same way. Blunt force trauma to the back of the head." The thought sickened her.

"And they think the murder weapon was from your shop?" Mason asked.

Clair shrugged. "I guess, but they won't find it." Her thoughts drifted back to the missing object from the phone table. That's because the murderer had probably already disposed of it. "It gets worse. They found a grey substance smeared over Roland Trent's shirt and it turned out to be grey icing. They believe it to be from the cupcakes you made for Mr Hapworth's thank you gift."

"Oh," Charlotte said sheepishly.

"What I can't work out is how that could have happened. I mean, you baked and iced them and I took them straight over with me last night and left them there when I went with Robert. The only thing I can think of is the murderer was still in the house."

"There has to be another explanation," Mason muttered.

Charlotte piped up. "There is."

Charlotte's head lowered, her teeth playing tug-o-war with her bottom lip. *Oh no, what have you done?*

"They weren't the only cupcakes I made yesterday. I wanted to get them right, so I made a few batches before you got there as testers. Suzi suggested putting them out in the shop, rather than wasting them, so I did and they all sold."

Mason's concerned gaze caught Charlotte's. "You have no idea who bought them?"

She shook her head. "No, it could have been anybody. But this is good," Charlotte continued, her voice getting progressively hyper as she spoke. "When you tell the police, they will have to start looking for someone else."

"Maybe," Clair said in an unconvincing tone. She peered around Charlotte and checked out the scene in front of the shop. The crowd appeared to have thinned but the police were still searching. *Thank goodness.*

"When I was out getting coffee earlier, I ran into Mrs Stevenson. First of all, she had no idea you'd been taken in for questioning. More importantly, she told me she saw Stella Roseamund in a heated discussion with Roland Trent the other day."

Clair raised an eyebrow. "Really? That *is* interesting. I think I need to have a chat with Stella."

"Listen, Clair, you've had a pretty rough morning. Why don't you let Mason take you home and I'll stay here and hold the fort?" Charlotte said.

Clair's mind was on information overload. *This is all too much.* "Maybe you're right."

"Of course I am." Clair held Charlotte tight as she hugged her goodbye. "I'll call as soon as I have news."

She smiled and nodded, turning to follow Mason to the car. *How can my life get so out of control so quickly?* She sat in silence, the events of the last twenty-four hours on repeat in her mind.

"You're awfully quiet," Mason said as he pulled up outside her house.

She smiled, embarrassment settled in her gut. "I'm sorry. I didn't mean to ignore you. I can't imagine how you must be feeling."

"I'm okay, but you know what will make you feel better?" he asked with a grin.

"No, what?"

"Coffee."

The word oozed from his lips and flooded her chest. *Oh, yes, hazelnut Nespresso.* "Definitely." She paused. *Will he expect to come in? Why wouldn't I want him to come in? After all, he does love a good coffee.*

"Would you care to join me?" she asked, praying her voice sounded calm.

"Thought you'd never ask." The glint in his eye eased the growing tension in her chest.

By the time she drained her coffee cup of the last drop, they'd relaxed into steady conversation. It was like talking to her best friend, only Mason was a lot easier on the eyes. If only she could block the world out and stay talking to Mason for the rest of the day.

Realising almost an hour and a half had gone by, Clair stood. "Thank you for listening. I feel much better now, but I really need to work out my next step in this fiasco if I'm going to clear my name."

His brow creased. "What are you talking about?"

Invigorated with renewed energy, she rattled off her to do list. "Well, for starters, I need to research more on this curse nonsense. I'd heard talk around town, but I didn't really take it seriously since I don't believe in curses or witchcraft or anything like that. Now I'm thinking I should have paid more attention. Then take a visit to Roland Trent's office. If his murder was related to your father's, then I should be able to find something incriminating. Dropping in on Stella will—"

"Woah, woah, slow down," Mason said, his chair scraping on the tiles as he stood. "I know you want to prove your innocence, and even though you don't have the best confidence in the Ashton Point Police Department, they are the trained professionals."

Trained professionals? Ha! "That's exactly what they said. I appreciate your concern, but if you think I'm going to trust my future, my sisters' futures and the survival of our business to the police, then you've got rocks in your head."

"So, you're going to put yourself in possible danger?" he asked through gritted teeth.

"I really don't think it will be that bad. What harm could it do? And if I can find information the police don't have, then I can clear my name quicker." She headed toward the door. "Thank you for helping out this morning, but I'm sure I can take it from here. Again, I'm really sorry for your loss and I appreciate you accepting my innocence," she said, holding the door open.

He stood frozen to the spot. "I don't suppose anything I will say is going to stop you."

She shook her head. "Nope."

"A beautiful woman like you should be protected, not putting her life at risk trying to catch a murderer. I would hate for you to get caught in the crossfire of whatever my father or this Roland Trent was mixed up in."

Clair stilled and her jaw dropped. *Beautiful woman?* Clair sucked in a deep breath, filling her lungs with much-needed air.

"Let me help you find the truth. You shouldn't be blamed for something you didn't do," he said, holding her gaze in his.

"I couldn't ask you to do that. You're mourning your father, the last thing you need is to be running around town with me playing detective."

"That's exactly what I need."

"Why? Why would you do that? You don't even know me."

"Although my father was really good at his job, I can imagine he may have trodden on a few toes. Someone wanted him dead. I'm pretty cluey when it comes to solving puzzles. It's what I've been doing most of my life. That's why I went into computer programming, and I'm good at my job."

She stood still and stared at him.

Charlotte's voice broke the tense silence as she strutted up the path to the porch. "Listen to him, Clair. If it weren't for Liam helping me, I might never have found out the truth."

Clair gasped, and her heart sank. "What are you doing here? You're supposed to be at the shop."

"Oh, they've finished the search. They removed a few items. Don't worry, I have a receipt for them. I've come to grab some of our replacement items so I can get started baking before the afternoon rush," Charlotte said, flitting past their dumbfounded expressions.

Clair followed. "I think we need to talk about a few things before you head back to the shop," she said, praying Charlotte would take the hint.

"Afraid I can't. I need to get back to work to fill some last-minute orders." Charlotte said, packing a canvas bag full of cooking equipment. "And besides, Mason said he would help you. I'm sure you two will be able to put your heads together and come up with a plan."

Mason smiled. "Charlotte's right. Two minds are better than one."

Clair sighed. "I suppose there could be some advantages to working closely together." No sooner had the words left her mouth her cheeks began to warm. Her eyes widened as if she knew her words had a double meaning.

"Great," Charlotte clasped her hands together. "It's settled. Now, if you'll excuse me." Charlotte trotted off in the direction of the front door, looking over her shoulder one last time. "Oh, and Mason, make sure my sister stays safe or you'll have to answer to me."

He gulped. "Yes, ma'am."

Clair rolled her eyes as a giggle erupted. "She can be so cheeky sometimes." Her words were interrupted by a strange sound that resembled *The Big Bang Theory*'s sitcom theme music.

"My apologies," Mason said as he scrambled for his phone. His gaze locked on the screen. A frown marred his face and his spine straightened.

"Is everything all right?" Clair asked concern etched in each word.

"Not sure. It's Stella." Tension twisted her insides as he rejected the call and returned it to his pocket. "I expect she's heard I'm back in town."

Clair's eyebrows shot up. "Why should that matter?"

"Apparently she's had her sights set on my father for a while. The last time I spoke to my dad he did mention they were getting serious. In a town this small, I'd expect it to spread through the grapevine like the chicken pox."

"Yes, I had heard something to that effect, but I wasn't sure if you knew," she said as she leant against the kitchen bench.

He folded his arms across his chest, pushing his pecs high. Her stomach did a little back-flip. "Are we in agreement? You'll let me help you?"

The gleam in his eyes caught her gaze. "Yes, like you said, two minds are better than one."

His arms dropped in a sigh. "Great. Now that's settled, may I make a suggestion?"

Clair nodded, eager to spend more time with him.

"If we divide our time we can get more accomplished." Her eagerness faded away by the second. "Since I have an in with Stella, maybe she could give me some insight into my father's activities, help me track his movements, and hopefully I'll get some answers that way."

That will be an interesting conversation.

"I'll go and see Stella under the pretence of discussing my father's estate and you—"

Clair jumped in, adrenaline pumping through her veins. "I'll jump on the Internet and do some in-depth research into this supposed curse to see what else I can find out and if there's any truth to it."

"There isn't," Mason said with a grin.

Clair held up her hands in a defensive manner. "I know. I know, but it wouldn't hurt to arm ourselves with as much information as possible." She glanced at the wall clock. "What do you say we meet back here in two hours?" She cringed. *Oh my, I sound like Trixie Beldon.*

Mason grabbed a pen and paper from the table and scribbled his mobile number down. "Here, take this. If you need me for anything, call."

She gifted him a huge smile. "Okay. In case I forget to say it later, thank you for believing me."

"You're welcome." He said with a smile before turning to leave.

Try as she might, she couldn't control the butterflies doing somersaults in her stomach.

Chapter Four

AS HE DROVE clear of Clair's house, Mason punched in Stella's number and hit speaker phone, dreading the pending conversation. His dad had brought Stella up to meet him almost six months ago, while on one of his "sure thing" real estate deals on the Gold Coast. It wasn't exactly the family reunion Mason had hoped for. The sickly smell of her cheap perfume, combined with his aftershave, had stuck with Mason long after they'd left.

Stella's drawl echoed down the line. "Hello."

"Stella, it's Mason," he said.

"Mason, about time," Stella snapped. "I know you are back in Ashton Point. Why did you ignore me in town today?"

He frowned. "Ignore you? What are you talking about?"

She huffed. "I saw you by the police station, right after your lovey-dovey cuddle with that meddling busy-body, Mrs Stevenson."

Mason's stomach dropped, picturing Stella dressed in her fake leopard print leggings, hot-pink Lycra top that was five sizes too small, and her thick layer of caked-on make-up. She was a clone image of Sylvia Fine, Fran Drescher's mother from *The Nanny*. Her face would crack if she attempted to smile. "Listen, Stella, as far as I'm concerned, it was more important to see the police and get a handle on the situation."

She suddenly spoke with a cunning edge to her words. "Mason, dearest, I should think it would be more important to come and comfort his poor grieving widow, wouldn't you?"

Widow? Mason could almost hear his heart beating against his ribcage as her words sunk in. *I did so not see that one coming.* Why on earth would his dad marry that dreadful woman?

"Did you hear what I said?" Stella asked smugly.

"Yes, I heard you, but I'm just trying to work out if you're delusional or drunk," Mason said as he leant his head back against the headrest.

"That's a dreadful thing to say," she said, faking hurt. "Especially to your step-mother."

"Step-mother," Mason yelled. His heart exploded in his chest and he felt his stomach roil at her pathetic tone. "I don't know what kind of sick joke you're trying to pull, but you will never be my step-mother. I'm sure he had his reasons for marrying you but I had a mother, one I loved very much."

"No joke. James and I were married last month when we were on one of his work trips in Sydney and I have the marriage certificate to prove it."

Marriage certificate? He momentarily pinched the bridge of his nose. "Well, I'm on my way over, so I guess we'll have time to chat about your recent nuptials."

Walking out onto the back patio of his father's house, Mason paused, holding down the nausea that welled in his stomach. Everywhere his gaze landed was fake. It was all for show. It was like an award-winning picture, straight out of *Home Beautiful* magazine. A pebbled, kidney-shaped pool off to the right set amongst a canopy of tropical, lush olive-green trees was his father's pride and joy. To the left, was a walk bridge leading to a sanctuary housing a four-post, double day bed, which was practically hidden amid a cluster of blue-purple blooming agapanthus. A gardener's paradise.

Mason's expression fell as he spotted Stella sitting at the end of the patio, champagne in one hand, a hors d'oeuvre in the other. Her head spun as he approached.

"Well, if it isn't my new son," Stella said as she swivelled in her chair. Her cold eyes stared straight through him.

Mason's heart jerked. "When hell freezes over, maybe."

Stella stood, pretending to wipe her tears. "I can't believe that McCorrson woman murdered my James."

Anger began to simmer in his chest. "She didn't."

"Oh, I don't know. If I'm to believe the paper, it seems the curse on that house got her as well."

"What do you mean 'as well'?" Mason asked, dubious of Stella's words.

She huffed, reaching for the champagne bottle to top up her glass. "That house is cursed, I tell you. I know you haven't lived here for a long time, but I would have thought the events of that house would have made it up to Surfers Paradise."

"I wouldn't believe everything you've read on the Internet."

Her icy-blue eyes widened and she gasped. "It wasn't just on the Internet. There's been talk around town, and not just recently. That house has a history and rumour has it that many years ago one of the previous owners went insane and died of a broken heart. She found her husband dead in the garden pool."

Mason's eyebrows shot up. "Dead in the garden pool?"

Stella nodded pursing her fake collagen injected lips at him. "That's what I've heard. It's the curse."

"You have a pretty good imagination, Stella, but I'm not here to talk about curses," he barked.

"No need to take that snappy tone with me." Stella frowned and slid a folder across the patio table in his direction. "Here you go, one marriage certificate as requested."

Repulsed by the thought, he scanned the document as quickly as possible, confirming they were indeed married. He steered the conversation to a much more interesting topic. "Actually, what can you tell me about Roland Trent?"

"Roland Trent? I'm not sure I know who that is," Stella said in a nervous tone.

Mason slid his hands into his pockets. *Really? Either you're lying or Mrs Stevenson is, and I know who I believe.*

"My mistake. So the fact that he was found murdered this morning shouldn't bother you."

"Murdered?" Stella paled, her jaw momentarily dropping in shock. "W-why should it bother me? As I said, I don't know who he is."

Mason forged ahead taking advantage of her lapse in concentration. "Then maybe you could shed a little light on James' movements over the past few weeks."

Stella stood there in a daze, her glassy gaze fixated on him.

"Stella? Stella," Mason called, finally breaking through her haze. "Can you tell me about James?"

"Very well. Take a seat," Stella said, flicking her manicured hands toward the empty chair.

Finally, I can get some answers. Mason thought, taking a seat opposite Stella.

"So what do you want to know?" she asked.

"How about his activities, for starters. Did he do anything out of the ordinary? Or change his pattern of behaviour?"

Stella paused then shook her head. "Not that I can think of. James was such a hard worker, you know, always out closing a deal. He normally worked out of his office here in Ashton Point but lately, he was working more and more in his office at Watson's Creek. Apparently, that's where the big bucks were or so he said. He was pretty much focused on work, that is, except for Thursday nights. He plays in the bowling league on Thursday evenings over at Watson's Creek."

"Excuse me?" Mason said, his drilling gaze cemented on Stella. "Bowling? My dad was bowling, as in tenpin bowling?"

He watched the forced movement of her throat as she swallowed. "Yes. Bowling," Stella said smugly. "I hear he was pretty good too."

How interesting. As far as Mason knew from communications with James several months back, he'd received a rotator cuff tear in his right shoulder in a charity golf match. How can one go bowling with an injured shoulder? "You didn't go with him?" Mason asked, his words slicing through the tense atmosphere.

"Listen, sweetheart," Stella said, leaning forward in her seat. "We may have been married, but we led our own lives. I had my interests, he had his."

Mason continued. "What else was he doing to occupy his time, *other* than bowling?"

Stella shot from her seat and stared daggers at Mason. "What are you implying?"

"Who said I was implying anything?"

"Whatever. I didn't keep tabs on him. I was his wife, not his mother. The only thing he was doing was some course in public relations, over at Watson's Creek TAFE. He was all about working to secure our future and all that. He was taking classes every

Monday evening, so he worked in his office in Watson's Creek 'til his course started. There were some Saturday workshops every now and then. I'm not really sure, he'd only just started it about a month ago. Now, if that is all."

Judging by Stella's incessant glare he knew he'd outstayed his welcome. "For now. I guess I'll be in touch," he said turning to leave. Mason didn't trust Stella one bit and his gut instincts were usually right, but he couldn't help feeling a little nervous about the blatant lies that easily escaped her lips.

An unnerving sensation skited around in Mason's stomach as he wrapped his knuckles on Clair's door. A feeling he wasn't accustomed to. He was still tossing his words around in his mind when the door flew open, startling him.

"Can I help you?" said a tall blonde woman, her eyebrows raised in question.

She wasn't Clair. "Um…is Clair home, my name is—"

"Mason Hapworth," she blurted, a smile spiked the corner of her lips.

He frowned. "Yes, how did you know?"

She folded her arms across her chest. "Clair mentioned that she met a handsome man this morning by the name of Mason Hapworth, and since I haven't seen you around town before, I'm guessing you must be him."

A surge of triumph ran up his spine. *Handsome? I'll take that.*

She rolled her lips together then said, "I was really sorry to hear about your father."

"Thank you."

She paused and rubbed her chin, looking him up and down. "Although, she didn't mention the glasses. You definitely have the Clark Kent look down pat."

"Excuse me?" he said, taken aback by her forthcoming manner.

She rolled her eyes. "You must know what I mean. Gorgeous guy tries to hide behind his sexy glasses. I'm Suzi, by the way, I work with Clair and Charlotte at CC's Simply Cupcakes."

"Pleasure to meet you, Suzi. Is Clair around?"

She gasped stepping back from the doorway. "Oh, my goodness, how rude of me. Please come in and I'll go get her for you. I was just about to leave anyway." Suzi quickly closed the door behind him and headed toward the kitchen. "Have a seat," she said, pointing toward the same kitchen chair he'd sat at earlier. "I'll go find her."

He'd forgotten what it was like to be on the receiving end of good old, small-town hospitality. It was something he missed terribly, living in the centre of a frenzied Surfers Paradise, especially during the summer months.

****

Three coffees and an hour and a half later, Clair sat crossed-legged on her bed, computer nestled in her lap, still engrossed in her Internet search. "Oh, my…no way," she muttered, her mind moving faster than her hand could write. Clair muttered to herself. "I did some research on the mansion, guess I wasn't looking in the right places." She should have kept digging, Google has an interesting way of hiding the very information you need, pages and pages into a search.

She'd been living in Ashton Point for three years and somehow the full history of the Sweets mansion had eluded her? While she didn't believe in curses, there had to be some truth to this new information. She'd found a few sites that mentioned a curse, but most were focused on the tragic fire of 1878. Clair flicked from site to site. "Far out. This one says a six-month-old baby died in the fire and its spirit is trapped in the house, while this one says it was a long-lost relative of Mrs Sweets who has escaped from jail."

Maybe the house is cursed.

And this one says no-one was killed in the fire, but it was started by a gas heater deliberately knocked over and igniting the woollen rug. Each site she read gave a different account. *What am I supposed to believe?* An odd sensation pricked the back of her neck and goose bumps bolted up her arms. Maybe she should have done a little more research before she put an offer in on the house. A cursed house can't be good for business.

Clair's head snapped up as a quiet knock at the door startled her. "Charlotte?"

"No, it's Suzi," she said cracking the door open a little. "Sorry for barging in like this, Charlotte was desperate for her design book. She's knee deep in flour and chocolate icing so she gave me her key to pop over to get it. Hope that was all right?"

Suzi was like a sister. She fit like a glove into their family unit, the only thing missing was the red hair. But she had the feistiness of a red-head. Clair smiled. "Of course, you know you're welcome here anytime."

"Charlotte did say she'd text you I was coming."

She did? Clair swiped her phone from the bedside table and checked. "Oops, here it is. Sorry about that. I was so engrossed with this curse business that I didn't even hear it go off."

Suzi pushed further into her room, a sly grin washed over her face as she sat on the end of Clair's bed. "I know you're busy, but there's a gorgeous man by the name of Mason here to see you, he's sitting in your kitchen."

Mason, back so soon and in my kitchen. She closed her eyes and flopped back against her cushy pillows. "So you've met him?"

Suzi nodded, her eyes shining like a child's on Christmas morning. "Sure did."

"I know I agreed to it, but I don't know how I'm supposed to work side-by-side with him?"

"Oh, come off it. He's not that bad. Actually, I think he's kinda cute." Suzi giggled.

"Exactly," Clair said her voice raising an octave. "He's more than 'kinda cute.'"

"If you *didn't* find him a tad attractive, there'd be something wrong."

Clair tried to put a lid on the personal tug-o-war her heart was playing and focus on the goal. Proving her innocence. "I know he said he wanted to help, but what if James' death really does have something to do with me? I don't want to be responsible for any more deaths in the Hapworth family. One is enough."

"You won't. Mason's a big boy. I'm sure he can take care of himself and if he can help, you should take it."

"I know you're right, but I can't afford any distractions right now."

"Come on, Clair. So, he's attractive. Surely, you've met attractive men before."

"Yes, but—"

Suzi shook her finger at Clair. "Don't play Miss Innocent with me, we've been friends way too long. If you think you're not going to be able to work with him, then I'd be happy to take your place and you can help Charlotte at the shop." Suzi's giggle grated on Clair's nerves.

No way.

Suzi continued without batting an eyelid. "You could always leave it up to Detective Anderson, but I can guarantee Mason is a much nicer option, and he smells way better. Even if he is only going to be here for a short time. What harm could it do?"

What harm, indeed?

Clair sighed in resignation. "Okay." *As long as I stay focused on the task and not the man, I'll be fine.*

Suzi bolted from the bed. "Great, I'm outta here. Good luck."

"Thanks," Clair said as she pulled her hair up and straightened her shirt. "I'm going to need more than luck." She looked toward the sky. "Grandma, if you can hear me I could really do with some help right about now."

Chapter Five

CLAIR GRABBED HER laptop from the bed and headed out to the kitchen, adrenaline pumping through her body. She paused a moment by the doorway as her eyes fell on Mason seated at the table. Her head spun like a giddy teenager's.

Suzi was right, he most definitely has the Clark Kent look happening. Her own words flitted through her mind. *But as long as I stay focused on the task and not the man I'll be fine.*

Clair squelched her growing desire for Mason and sucked in a deep, painful breath. "Mason," she said, stepping into the kitchen.

His head spun and his eyes widened. She flinched at the dubious look in his eyes. *Gee, I didn't think I looked that bad.*

"Clair, nice to see you again. Suzi let me in, I hope you don't mind?"

She smiled. "Of course not."

He nodded at her laptop. "How did you do researching the curse?"

Now, there's a topic she could definitely talk about. She pulled out a chair and joined him at the table, ignoring her stepped-up pulse rate. "Actually, there was more information than I expected." She re-opened her laptop at the articles and turned it in Mason's direction. "It all seems to stem from the fire of 1878. As you can see, it appears there are a number of articles, each with a different version of the fire and each with a different victim. The curse is mentioned in a few, but the truth is anyone's guess."

Mason frowned as his gaze searched each article. "I see what you mean."

Clair couldn't take her eyes off him. She found herself wondering if he ever wore contact lenses. If he did, she'd be able to see his gorgeous eyes shine, instead of being hidden behind those thick-rimmed glasses. *Focus.*

"What did you find out about Stella and Roland Trent," she asked, moving from the table to the coffee machine. *More coffee?* Her energy levels were already off the scale, she'd be climbing the walls if she had any more caffeine. She opted for a glass of filtered water instead.

"I guess the question should be 'what *didn't* I find?'" he said closing her laptop.

"Excuse me?" she said with a raised eyebrow.

"As you know, my father and Stella have been an item." He waited for her acknowledgment before continuing. "Seems they got married about a month ago."

Clair's jaw dropped. "No way. How did they keep that a secret in this town?" She could see the disdain on his face.

"I'm pretty sure half the words she spoke were lies. According to Stella, my dad went ten pin bowling every Thursday evening, which I know is impossible since he tore the rotator cuff in his right shoulder in a golf tournament."

"Ouch, that would be painful," Clair said, her stomach squirming.

Mason nodded. "Exactly. Either she's lying or my dad was lying to her about his whereabouts on Thursday evenings. Then she informs me he was also taking a public relations course every Monday evening and some Saturdays at Watson's Creek. Now, if he lied about the bowling, he could have lied about that as well. Either way, it needs further investigation."

Clair rubbed her chin, digesting each word as he spoke. "And Roland Trent?"

"She denied ever knowing him, which we both know is a lie if we are to believe Mrs Stevenson, and I do."

A renewed energy bolted Clair into action. "All the more reason to check out Roland Trent's office. There has to be something in there that can link him to either James or Stella." She threw her bag over her shoulder and grabbed her keys. "Are you coming?"

Mason stood, concern plastered over his expression. "To Roland Trent's office? Do you think that's wise?"

"Yep. It may be the only way to find the truth and we might be able to put those computer skills of yours to good use."

Mason frowned. "How are we supposed to get into his office? For all we know, the police have blocked it off."

She giggled, heading for the front door. "I have an in with the doorman. You see, we came to the rescue with an awesome mermaid cupcake display for his daughter's eighth birthday not so long ago so he owes me. We'll say we're looking at a location for a new business. It can't be helped if we just happen to head into the wrong door while we're there." A cheeky grin spread across his face and she knew she'd scored bonus points. "Shall we?" she asked holding the door open.

"It sounds like I'm not going to change your mind, even if I wanted to," Mason said as he brushed past her.

"That's right," she said pulling the door to behind her.

"Would you like me to drive?" Mason asked. "We could always use it as another cover. You know, showing me the sights of Ashton Point. I'm sure it's changed a lot since I lived here ten years ago."

"Sure." Her words bombarded her thoughts once again. *As long as I stay focused on the task and not the man, I'll be fine.*

By the time Mason pulled up outside Sampson Office Building in Watsons Creek, Clair's nerves were as jumbled as a bowl of tagliatelle pasta. Mason had made small talk most of the way. The more conversation he made the more she felt him placating her, as if he was steering clear of any real conversation that involved him sharing about himself. She couldn't really blame him. It's not like he owed her an explanation or anything. Losing your father under such questionable circumstances would rattle anyone's cage.

"What if you can't find the answers you're looking for?" Mason asked as they headed toward the entrance.

"Us McCorrson women are pretty resilient. I'll think of something." Clair winked in Mason's direction, her heart doing a little hiccup as a cute dimple surfaced on his right cheek. "Just follow my lead and what could go wrong?"

Clair mentally crossed her fingers and prayed. *Please let me find the answers I'm looking for.*

She pushed through the double glass doors, breathing a sigh of relief when her gaze fell on Arthur sitting at the reception desk. Clair turned on her best professional smile and sashayed up to the counter. "Arthur, it's so good to see you again. How is that beautiful daughter of yours?"

Arthur's eyes widened with tenderness as he stood. "Clair. She's doing great, as usual. I've been so worried about you with all this murder and curse business running around town. Anyone who would believe you would ever hurt someone has rice bubbles in their head for brains."

Relief bloomed in her chest at his vote of confidence. "Thank you, Arthur. It's nice to have at least one other person in Ashton Point that believes in my innocence."

Arthur gasped, his jaw dropping. "Nonsense, there's plenty of people who believe in you." His gaze caught Mason's in passing. "Can I help you, sir?"

"Excuse my rudeness," Clair said, her gaze flitting sideways. "This is Mason Hapworth. James Hapworth's son. He drove down from Surfers Paradise when he heard about his father's death."

"Nice to meet you," Mason said holding his hand out.

Arthur stepped out from behind his desk and greeted Mason. "I'm sorry to hear about your father."

"Thank you."

"I hope you don't think this young lady had anything to do with his murder?" Arthur snapped, crossing his arms across his chest. Clair's knees wobbled like jelly as Mason's magnetic gaze glued her to the spot.

"No, I don't believe for one moment that this gorgeous woman would hurt a fly, let alone kill someone and I'm doing my best to help keep her mind distracted." He smiled at Clair and her heart momentarily stopped.

Distracted? As long as I stay focused on the task and not the man, I'll be fine.

Mason continued oblivious to her frozen status. "As I was saying to Clair earlier today, when things aren't always going as planned, I like to focus on work."

"Is that so," Arthur said with a smirk. He finally returned his attention to Clair. "What can I do for you, Clair?"

With her attention momentarily frozen on Mason, Arthur's words were like a muffled record straining to be heard. *Gorgeous woman?*

Mason cleared his throat and took a step closer to the counter. "I mentioned to Clair this morning that I was looking at starting my own computer business here in town and I thought since she'd done some research on the local real estate market, she might be able to point me in the right direction. I was right, 'cause here we are."

You were? Clair raised her eyebrows and glared at Mason. Giddiness swept through her. *How did I miss that bit of information?*

"Isn't that right, Clair?" Mason asked, turning to face her square on. His eyes widened and his lips suddenly moved without a sound. "Follow my lead," he mouthed.

Realising her blunder, she shook the cobwebs from her mind and once again focused on the task. *That's the last time I let my guard down. Time to prove my innocence.*

She beamed a gentle smile at both men. "That's right and this is the place to be. This building right here is going to be *the* business hub before you know it. I thought while Mason was in town, I'd bring him down to look at some of the available office spaces I'd heard about. I'm sure they're exactly what he's looking for. Would that be all right, Arthur?"

"Normally, the real estate agent likes to be with the client when they are showing them through the empty offices," Arthur said in a matter-of-fact manner.

Clair's stomach bottomed out. *Oh no, he's not going to let us in. What now?*

Mason piped up before Clair could utter a word. "You are absolutely right and normally I would head there first, but it was a spur-of-the-moment decision. Clair and I have had a pretty rough time and we both needed something to get our minds off what's been going on. Couldn't you cut us some slack, just this once?"

Clair found her voice. "It would mean the world to me, Arthur."

The growing tension was like walking on eggshells and she held her breath. Arthur's lips turned upward into a warm smile. "That should be no problem. After all, what are friends for?" He handed her a bunch of keys. "Here you go. These will get you into the empty offices on level three. There are only four currently available."

The breath escaped her lips. "Thanks, Arthur, you're a real friend," Clair said as she grabbed the keys and headed for the lifts with Mason hot on her heels. "Boy, that was close," she whispered.

Her heart was racing like a galloping horse inside her chest. Now to get down to business. Clair's gaze casually scanned the index board by the lift controls. *Roland Trent and Associates, Level Eight.* Mason had already pressed the button for level three when she turned to him. "We need level eight," she whispered.

He looked down at her with his enticing gaze. "Yes, I know, but Arthur will be expecting the lift to stop at three and if it doesn't, what's to stop him coming over to check? We get off at level three and walk the stairs for the rest."

She balked at the thought. "Five flights of stairs?"

Mason smirked. "What's the matter, a little out of shape are we?"

Out of shape…Ha! I'll show you out of shape. A twinge of annoyance niggled at the back of Clair's mind. "Not a problem. You lead the way and I'll keep up."

Clair's lungs begged for air. Each foot moved one stair after the other, until she took the last step to level eight. She'd kept pace with Mason up the stairwell, ignoring the razor-cutting burn in her legs. The sideways movement of his tight derriere hadn't even been able to distract her from the pain. *Oh, my goodness, how did I get so out of shape? Charlotte's cupcakes, that's how. I promise if I get out of this mess alive I'm cutting down to two cupcakes a day, and joining a gym.*

"How you doing back there?" Mason asked as they exited the stairwell.

Clair noticed that Mason had barely cracked a sweat. "Okay, I give in. How are you not even breathless after that climb?"

"Jealous?" he said. Spinning around to face her, he continued walking backward down the corridor.

"Hardly. You're a computer programmer, right?" He nodded. "You sit behind a computer all day and play with a keyboard. How are you not exhausted?"

He stopped suddenly. *Ahhhh.* Clair's jelly legs ignored the message her brain was sending. *Stop…stop…please stop.* She found herself pitching forward into his arms. Her adrenaline-charged body connected with his and it was as if they were suddenly locked in a moment of time together. His muscles tensed as she gripped his shoulders while he held her gaze in his.

He swallowed. "Are you all right?"

Sure. My heart feels like a ticking time-bomb, my legs feel like they have just walked across the Nullarbor Plain and I'm in the arms of a man that scrambles my thoughts. Why wouldn't I be all right?

Clair pushed her tense hands off his taut chest. "Of course. I guess those stairs really did a number on my legs." She shook her legs praying the pins and needles would evaporate sooner rather than later. "You still haven't answered my question. How are you not exhausted?"

His brow creased. "I work out. I'm into computer programming and I love it, but a friend of mine who works in the same building as me is into designing games. Not with lots of killing or over-the-top violence, but he creates different types of fantasy worlds that teach people to build societies where they can be self-sufficient and live off the land. That includes defending themselves. He set up a gym in the basement of our building and he lets me use it to work out while he tests moves for his games with his workmates."

I'd like to test your moves. Where on earth did that come from? *Focus on the task, not the man.* Clair felt a little more of her heart soften toward this man. "What an amazing job."

"Yeah." He turned and continued down the corridor toward Roland Trent's office, Clair following. "Thank you for going along with my little charade earlier."

Clair's brow creased. "Charade?"

"Opening a computer business here in town. I just went with your lead and it was the first thing that popped into my head." He stopped outside Roland's office.

"No problem." Of course, it was all an act. As if he would leave the high life of Surfers Paradise. *I swear, from this moment on, my focus is now 100% on clearing my name and nothing else.*

With a renewed sense of purpose, she rolled her shoulders back, sucked in a deep breath and took a step forward, then froze. "The door," she whispered. "It's ajar."

She leant her ear against it, straining to hear signs of life inside. Mason joined her, his lips inches from hers. His spicy aftershave bled into her chest and she held her breath. *Focus, focus, focus.* She closed her eyes and listened harder, it was all she could do to stop herself from pushing up on her toes and kissing him.

"I can't hear a thing, can you?" she asked Mason.

He shook his head. "No, but just keep your eyes and ears open for the unusual."

Clair's nerves were like elastic bands, ready to snap at a moment's notice. She eased the door open, her gaze scanning for any unwanted guests. "It's empty," she said moving farther into the office. Mason semi-closed the door behind them.

"Let's be quick about this," Mason whispered as his gaze fell on the computer. "We don't want Arthur to come looking for us."

"Agreed. The clue to my freedom could be here, so let's get to work. I'll search the filing cabinet, you see if you can find anything on his computer."

Mason nodded and went to work, his fingers moved at lightning speed across the keys.

Electricity burned her chest as the filing draw released under her pull. "Yes." She wanted to jump up and do a high five in the air. "He's got a pretty tight security lock on this, which tells me he's hiding something. It isn't going to be easy to crack, even with my advanced skills, but I'll give it a shot," Mason said, his eyes glowed with determination.

Clair worked her way through the files, the unknown names blurring into one. The tapping of Mason's fingernails became a distant drone. She'd just about given up when her gaze spotted exactly what she'd been looking for. *Jackpot.*

Her stomach tightened. Stella Roseamund. *Maybe this will tell me why you lied to Mason.* She whipped the file out and her heart sank. *Empty? Was there something in here worth killing for?*

Clair closed the file and turned to see if Mason had more luck than she did. Uneasiness crept into Clair's gut. Before she could utter a word, a high-pitched ding signalling the arrival of the elevator, followed by muffled voices drifting down the corridor. A sense of foreboding came over her as the voices loomed closer.

Mason shot from his chair and darted toward the oncoming sound. Peering through the ajar door, he had a perfect view of the elevator. "It's Detective Anderson and Arthur and they're headed this way."

Of course, they are. This is just going from bad to worse. Panic rose in her chest. "What are we going to do?" she asked, her legs frozen to the spot. In a matter of seconds, she'd be able to add breaking and entering to her supposed list of misdemeanours.

Mason carefully closed the door and looked around the office. "Quick, through here," he said as he grabbed her hand, dragging her toward an adjoining door.

Please be open, she prayed. It was, and he pushed her through.

They stood like statues against the wall. Her breathing was laboured. Mason had left the door open an inch to listen, but it was Clair's pummelling heart that filled her ears. *Breathe, just breathe.*

Detective Anderson's commanding voice boomed through the small office. "Thank you. That will be all. I'll see myself out."

"Very well, Detective," Arthur said.

Clair leant her head back against the wall and squeezed her eyes shut. *Please don't find anything that points to me.* Clair felt butterflies in her stomach. The trouble was, she couldn't be sure it was the fear of being caught or the touch of Mason's hand in hers. Her gaze met his warm and reassuring eyes and for a moment she was lost in the deep depth of his gaze. Mason stiffened, the trance broken by the recorded voice of James Hapworth.

"Roland, are you there? Pick up, if you are...I'm meeting her tonight and I'm sure I can persuade her to change her mind. If she doesn't there are other avenues we can explore so don't worry, I'll handle it. You just keep your end of the deal and everything will turn out as planned. Trust me."

Clair's mind raced. *Meeting who? Me? What other ways? And if it was me, why did he want me to change my mind?*

The tension was cut by Detective Anderson's sharp tone. "Sounds like you and James Hapworth had unfinished business, hey, Roland."

Was that unfinished business me?

Clair glanced sideways at Mason and her heart melted at the genuine concern etched in his expression. The familiar glide of the filing cabinet drawer sent instant panic shooting through her chest. Her gaze dropped to Stella's file, which she held tight in her hands. *Oh my gosh, how could I have been so silly?* Now they could add breaking and entering *and* stealing.

"Anderson, here. Fine, I'm on my way."

Clair's heartbeat picked up a few notches. The distant ping of the elevator confirmed Anderson's departure. A burning roar worked its way from her chest to her throat, a reminder to breathe.

Mason, still holding her hand, squeezed it. "Let's get out of here. I don't know about you but I could use a stiff drink."

"Sounds good to me."

Chapter Six

THEY'D MADE IT out without incident and with Arthur none the wiser. "I can't believe I have more questions than answers," Clair said, pushing her empty beer glass to the centre of the table.

Mason took another bite of his burger, a trickle of sauce tickling his chin. "Pardon me," he said wiping it with a napkin. *Gee, talk about clumsy. I can't even eat a burger in front of her without wearing it on my face.*

Clair smiled and swallowed the last bite of her burger. "It's okay. That's what makes Charlie's burgers so good. The sauce."

"This really is an amazing burger," he said, eyeing Clair as they sat in the beer garden at The Corner2 Pub. Mason's tastebuds were in heaven, not to mention his stomach. The tender meat was seasoned with tangy spices and the bun was so fresh it sang in his mouth.

"Told you," she said rocking her empty glass. "Best burgers in town."

He nodded toward her glass. "I didn't peg you for a beer woman."

"Sorry to disappoint you," she said, her hurt tone startling him.

You idiot, way to put your foot in it. "No disappointment at all. In fact, I like that you prefer beer. There's something about a woman who can hold her own with the men." The cutest crimson blush worked its way up her neck. He didn't think it was possible for her to be more beautiful. *I really need to get out from behind my computer screen more often.* He was wrong.

No time to act like a nerd now. "Are you sure there wasn't anything else in the files of interest?" he asked.

She sighed and shook her head. "No, like I said, there was only the empty file with Stella's name on it."

"Look on the bright side. That confirms they did know each other."

"Yes, but why was she lying about knowing him?" Mason felt Clair's frustration from where he was sitting. "What did she have to do with Roland Trent, and why lie about it unless…"

"Unless what?" he asked with a raised eyebrow.

"Unless it has something to do with his murder?"

The ominous word hung over them and they continued to eat in silence. The pub ambience was buzzing with a welcoming, friendly vibe, different to the pubs back home in Surfers Paradise.

He tensed and chuckled to himself. *How would I know, it's not like going to pubs is a regular event back home.* He was kind of a loner and hadn't had reason to socialise outside the office or gym, until now. This would be his first in a long time.

"Something funny?" Clair asked.

He shuffled in his seat, "No, I was just thinking about how nice this place is." His gaze watched Clair as she looked around. The warmth that filled her eyes gnawed at his heart. Mason lived and worked in Surfers Paradise, but the connection was never strong enough to call it home.

"It is a pretty special place. I can't see myself living in any other town," she said. "Although." Her brow creased. "If I don't find out the answers I need, the only place around here I'll be seeing is the inside of a jail cell."

His gut twisted in knots. *Not if I can help it.*

She bit her bottom lip and he could almost see the wheels turning in her head. He finished the last gulp of his beer. The icy liquid slid down his throat, cooling his insides.

She continued. "Tell me if I have this right. We know Roland knew Stella, otherwise why have a file on her, but don't know if and why she lied about meeting him. We know Stella believes James was bowling and we know that isn't true because of his injured shoulder. So, either James was lying to Stella or she was lying to us. Judging by the phone call, we know he was meeting a woman that night, the question is which woman?"

"It could have been you, but who's to say it wasn't Stella or someone else? And if it was you, what did he want to change your mind about? The settlement or the mansion or something completely different? Either way I think Roland is involved in some way. How am I doing so far?"

"Pretty on point, but now we have more questions. Maybe Roland was the other buyer. Sounds like both Stella and Roland had dealings with James, but were they enough to force one of them to kill him? And if Roland killed James, who killed Roland?"

"Good points, all of them. Ones that we need to find the answers to." Frustration settled in the base of his gut.

"I don't trust Stella one iota," Clair said, leaning back in her chair. "I think we should speak to someone in this bowling league, anyway. Just to confirm one way or another. It's a place to start."

"Agreed. I'll make some calls and see what I can find out."

She nodded and paused, her gaze falling on her empty plate. "Um, I could..." The wall clock above the bar chimed and she froze in her seat. He paused, his gaze holding hers steady. Clair checked her watch. "Oh, darn. I was supposed to be home thirty minutes ago to help Charlotte. She's designing a new line of fantasy cupcakes and wanted to run her ideas by me. I'm sorry to cut this short."

He sat and watched her wispy, red curls bounce around her slender neck. He'd been so focused on work lately it'd been a while since he'd dated or wanted to kiss a woman, but he'd make an exception for Clair. *Snap out of it, man. The objective is to clear Clair of murder, not find a date.* "No problem. How about I come by tomorrow around nine and we can pick up where we left off?"

She gifted him with a smile that spoke to his heart. "I'd like that."

"I still can't believe you went to Roland Trent's office yesterday," Charlotte said as Clair walked into the kitchen heading straight to the coffee machine. "Thank goodness Detective Anderson didn't find you."

"Tell me about it." The thought sent goose bumps fanning across her skin. "Next time, I'll be more careful."

Charlotte raised her eyebrows. "Next time?"

Clair held her warm coffee, her chilled hands beginning to thaw by its touch. "You can't expect me to stop looking for answers. You of all people should understand."

"I know, but how about keeping me in the loop? Just in case I need to bail you out of jail, I'll know why," Charlotte said with a cheeky glint in her eye.

"Deal." The love for her sister blossomed in her heart.

"You didn't have to come home last night, you know? I could have finished the cupcake designs by myself."

"I know." Clair felt a momentary pang in her gut. Guilt? "I said I would help and I thought it only fair to let you know what Mason and I found out."

"How was dinner with *Mr Perfect*?" Charlotte asked.

Charlotte's question triggered mouth-watering images of Mason. *Mr Perfect, indeed. Perfect lips. Perfect hair. Perfect butt.* He even looked gorgeous with a dribble of sauce down his chin.

"Oh, no," Charlotte said smirking at her sister. "You've got it bad."

Clair frowned. Charlotte looked as if she'd just solved the world's poverty problems. "What on earth are you talking about?"

"You like him." Charlotte chuckled popping a spoonful of Coco Pops into her mouth.

"Well, of course I like him, he's a nice guy, he's helping prove my innocence and he just lost his father for goodness sake." Clair silently prayed. *Drop it, please drop it, Charlotte.*

Charlotte pursed her lips and frowned. "You know that's not what I mean."

Clair's breath caught in the back of her throat. Her head hurt with all the reasons why she shouldn't like him, but her heart wanted what it wanted, and it wanted Mason. "Okay, you win," she said joining her at the table, her head in her hands. "I confess. I really like Mason."

"Really? I'd like to be around when the town gets a hold of that piece of information," Liam said, leaning against the kitchen doorframe.

Clair's head shot up and her heart lurched as she watched the grin on Liam's face grow. She gasped and swallowed the golf-ball-sized lump in her throat. "Liam you cannot repeat that to anyone, you hear me?" She barrelled toward him like an approaching storm halting inches from his face. "Promise me you'll keep it to yourself," she said stabbing her finger in his firm chest. Clair was seconds from turning her sister's status to single. "It's hard enough working alongside him, if the town got a hold of it I'd never hear the end of it."

His eyebrows shot up and he held up his hand in defence. "Okay, okay. Geeze, I was just kidding around. Honest."

"You had better be." Her logical brain knew he could be trusted, but her gut was telling her something entirely different. Clair shuffled back to her seat, her heart deflating. "Why is it you had to walk in at that exact moment?"

"Yes, sweetie, why are you here so early? Don't you remember? Even though I'm not rostered on today, Clair and I have to head into the shop this morning to work on cupcake designs for the

Founder's Day Gala dinner this weekend. I thought we were catching up later for lunch," Charlotte said between mouthfuls. Liam took the seat beside Charlotte and huddled close to give her a peck on the cheek.

Oh no, Clair felt a chill run up her spine as Liam's face fell. "What's happened?" she asked. *Please don't let there be a body inside the shop this time.*

Liam stared from one sister to the other, concern clouding his deep, chocolate-brown eyes.

Charlotte frowned. "Spit it out, sweetheart. Now you're starting to worry me."

"Have either of you seen the paper this morning?"

It was at that moment Clair noticed he had one arm hidden below the table. An imaginary hand squeezed her throat. *Stay calm, it could be nothing. Maybe there's a sale on baking equipment and he doesn't want us to miss a bargain.*

"I know you've got a copy, otherwise why would you mention it. Just show us, Liam," Clair said, bracing herself for another onslaught of lies.

"Okay, at least you're sitting down."

"That bad, huh," Charlotte asked, tension marring her expression.

Liam shrugged. "I'll let you be the judge." He held the paper up to show another devastating headline next to a giant picture of Clair six years ago at an animal activist rally looking like she was about to murder someone.

Cupcake Killer Has Killed Before!

Clair puffed her cheeks and blew out a long breath of air and her heart sank like a stone in water. "I don't believe this," she said, pulling the paper from Liam's hands. Her gaze ran over the article, each word a knife in her chest. "First the article yesterday and now this!"

"This is ridiculous," Charlotte said, her tense expression echoing Clair's own. "That rally was yonks ago and you did not kill anyone, at least not that I can remember."

Clair licked her lips and swallowed back the urge to swat Charlotte over the head with the newspaper. "Of course I didn't. Things got a little out of hand and I happened to get caught in the middle, but I did not kill anyone. Although this picture makes me look like a deranged killer."

"The article says you attacked the police, and when they tried to restrain you, you retaliated and lashed out, knocking a man unconscious who later died in hospital."

That is not true. Why do people insist on printing lies about me? Was it her, or was the air in the kitchen getting thicker? "I'm well aware of what the article says, Liam, but it's wrong. Completely and utterly wrong. Sure I was there, and I did my fair share of protesting. Peacefully, I might add. I was nowhere near the violence and I did not attack anyone, let alone the police."

Adrenaline coursed through her veins as the familiar name of the journalist left the bitter taste of disgust in her mouth. *Christina Jacobs, what did I ever do to you?* Clair closed her eyes against the sudden rush of anger.

"Clair?" Charlotte said, her tone edged with concern. "Are you all right?"

Emotion clogged her voice. "No, I am not all right." Her eyes flew open and she sucked a deep breath into her lungs. "Once people see this, they'll think I'm a murderer for sure." Clair surged from her seat, the high-pitched scrape of the chair legs on the tiles ran shivers down her spine. "I'm not giving in that easy. Yesterday was pretty much a dead end. I think it's time I paid Christina Jacobs an impromptu visit," she said storming, from the room. "Don't worry, I'll keep you posted," Clair called over her shoulder as she disappeared into her room.

Clair racked her brain trying to remember what she'd done to offend Christina, but her mind blanked. "I just don't get it," she muttered as she put the finishing touches on her make-up. Clair pulled her bushy red hair back into a ponytail at the base of her neck. Dressed in a sea-green, chiffon top, three-quarter, black jeggings and white-wedge heels, she took one final glance in the mirror and smiled. *I don't scrub up half bad.*

Her bedside clock read 8:05 a.m. Plenty of time to see Christina and be back before Mason arrives at nine. She grabbed the newspaper, her handbag, and headed out.

By the time Clair pulled into a car bay outside the Ashton Point Chronicle, her thoughts were focused solely on why Christina had it in for her. Clair pushed through the door, her wavy red ponytail flying around in the briny sea breeze. Approaching the empty counter, she tapped the bell several times, her impatience getting the better of her. "Hello... Hello, is anyone here?" she called.

"Hang on a second." A stark male voice called from an office to her right.

Her pulse sped. Drumming her fingernails on the counter, impatience boomed in the base of her belly.

"Clair? What are you doing here so early?" Daniel said as he approached, carrying a steaming mug of fresh vanilla-scented coffee. Her second favourite coffee flavour behind hazelnut.

"I think you know very well what I'm doing here." She flung the paper on the counter open at the damning article.

"Oh, that." Daniel shrugged. "It's just a story. Christina likes to add her own flair to her editorials. Papers sell when there's a little controversy."

"Controversy? Like the controversy you created when you printed that bogus story about Charlotte poisoning her cupcakes at Beth and Lincoln's wedding?"

Hurt marred his expression. "Hey, my sources were correct at the time. Anyway, everything turned out all right in the end. Charlotte was cleared."

"No thanks to you." She pointed to the paper once more. "This is a pack of lies. Next, she'll have me pinned as Roland Trent's murderer as well. Where is Christina? I want to talk to her."

He grimaced and shook his head. "I'm afraid she's not here. You'll have to come back later. She's over at the police station with Detective—"

Clair snatched the paper and spun on her heel. She didn't wait for him to finish. The sooner she reached the police station, the sooner she could sort out this mess.

Clair walked double-time down the street. The morning sun was already warming the pavement under her feet. A stream of sweat trickled down Clair's neck into her cleavage. *Great, that's all I need, sweat patches on my chest. Not really the look I was going for.*

Clair ran her clammy hands down her jeggings and by the time she got to the police station steps, she was perspiring like she'd just finished a hot yoga class. She had visible wet patches under her arms and thanks to her sweaty neck, the hair that had worked its way loose from her ponytail was now in ringlets. Her insides were simmering and it wasn't just from the burning sun. *I swear, Christina, if I run in to Mason looking like a wet rag I am not going to be very happy.*

She burst through the station doors and a wave of icy air brushed over her. Relief soared through her body. *Oh, thank goodness.* She focused on the tall blonde at the counter while she let the cool air seep through her limbs.

Christina had made it very clear when they'd moved to Ashton Point that she wasn't afraid to speak her mind. Apparently, that's what makes a great reporter, at least that's what she tells everyone. For as long as Clair could remember she'd never been one to go unnoticed and today was no different. A blonde bombshell straight out of a 1940s Hollywood movie. A jealous streak worked its way into Clair's tight chest. Christina was expertly showing off her curvaceous figure in a semi-see-through cream blouse and a tight, navy pencil skirt, exposing luscious legs that went all the way up to her armpits.

Clair shook her head and joined her at the counter. "Christina, Daniel said I might find you here. Would you mind telling me why you would print such lies about me on the front page of your paper?"

"Excuse me," Christina said as she spun, brushing her long blonde locks over her shoulder. "I don't know what you're talking about?"

Clair wanted to wipe that smug look off her face with her own newspaper. "Oh, really," she said pulling the paper from her bag. "This is what I'm talking about." She held up the front page. "These lies. I want to know where you got your information from, because it's all wrong."

"A reporter never reveals their source."

"That's if you even have a source," she snapped throwing the newspaper on the counter.

Christina's ice-blue eyes narrowed. "Are you calling me a liar?"

Clair blinked away tears of frustration. "If the shoe fits. Tell me who you got your information from."

Christina leaned in leering at Clair. "Like I said, a reporter never reveals their source."

"That's because there is no source, is there? You fabricated false details of this old story to make me look like a murder. To make everyone think I was capable of being a cold-blooded killer. Why? Why would you print this before finding out the truth from me? Unless you had another reason to print that nonsense."

Christina straightened her back and stepped away from Clair. "You don't know what you're talking about. A reporter's source must be protected at all costs."

Clair's eyes widened in surprise at Christina's defensive manner. "I did not kill James Hapworth or Roland Trent and no amount of lies you print will cover the truth, and I *will* find the truth, Christina, you can count on it."

"Ladies, please." Their heated discussion had caught the attention of the police receptionist, Alison.

She stepped up to the counter. "I know you're both upset but you need to calm down. Throwing accusations won't help anyone."

"I'll take it from here, Alison." A man said from behind her and she whirled around to see Detective Anderson standing, arms crossed with a disgruntled expression on his face. "I think that's enough of a display in my police station, don't you, ladies?"

An iron fist squeezed Clair's chest. She could barely breathe around the anger that bled through her system. She opened her mouth to speak but her words were cut short by Christina's fake tone.

"Of course. How utterly rude of me." She turned her phoney apologetic eyes on Clair. "Please forgive me, Clair? You're right. I should have come to you with the story first to check the facts before sending it to print."

What the...? Clair cocked her eyebrow at Christina, wondering why the change of heart.

"I guess I let my inquisitive journalist streak get the better of me. Speaking of facts..." The sparkle returned to Christina's eyes. "Detective, while we're here, why not give us an update? So Clair, here, can be guaranteed I'll get the next story right."

Facts, yes. Did he go back to Roland's office and find Stella's file? Clair could almost hear her heart beating in the silence while she waited for his response. "Yes, the least you could do is tell us what you have found so far. After all, it is my life on the line."

"Actually, I don't have to tell you anything, but in the spirit of cooperation, I think it's best to keep all parties apprised of developments. Mason Hapworth insisted that you be kept in the loop." He sighed and ushered them over to the left side of the foyer out of earshot of the general public.

Clair's insides warmed and this time it wasn't from the heat of the day. *Thank you, Mason.*

"At present, we can confirm that both men were killed by a blow to the back of the head with some sort of rounded object. It looks like the same or similar weapon was used but we haven't had any luck recovering it. It's not looking hopeful, considering the amount of old furniture and trinkets left in the house by Mrs Sweets when she passed. The murderer could have used an object from the house and disposed of it by now and we'd never know. We're still working on the connection of the two men." His gaze zoned in on Clair. "A search of Roland Trent's office turned up one bit of interesting information."

Clair took a deep breath to squelch the nervous tension firing through her veins. "It did?" *The phone message.*

"Yes, a recorded message from James about a meeting with a woman. At first we thought it related to you, Clair."

"Me?"

"Yes, but we've since ruled you out since the date on the tape was the day before the murder. We've conducted searches of both Hapworth's offices and came up empty."

Her relief was short lived. No murder weapon, and no mention of his marriage to Stella. *Did he even know they were married?*

"No incriminating evidence was found at either place or on his computers. We've confirmed he only owns the two laptops we found, but we're hoping we'll be able to find his mobile phone at his house. We're just waiting on a warrant now."

"A search warrant?" Christina asked, her pen still scribbling words on her note pad.

"Apparently, he shacked up with Stella Roseamund shortly before his death and she has refused us entry without probable cause and a search warrant."

"Well, considering she is his widow, she has every right to refuse you entry," Clair said.

Both Christina and Detective Anderson looked at her as if she'd just confessed.

"What?" They said in unison.

"So, you didn't know? They were married recently. He didn't even have the decency to tell his own son." Clair paused and suddenly became aware of Christina's drilling gaze.

"What else do you know?" Detective Anderson asked in a frustrated tone.

She frowned. *Like I'm going to tell you two. You'll probably twist it around and make me look even guiltier.* "It isn't my place to do your job for you, Detective, but I suggest you have a good long talk to Stella. I'm sure she knows more than she's letting on about James' whereabouts over the past few months and maybe she might be able to give you some answers regarding Roland Trent." She turned her gaze on Christina. "Now, you've got someone new to torment." She hiked her bag up on her shoulder. "If you'll both excuse me, I think I've had enough excitement for one morning."

Before they could stop her, Clair was out the door and on the way back to her car. Her fists clenched at her sides. *At least that little tidbit of information about Stella should keep those two off my back for a while.*

Clair was interrupted by the trilling of her mobile phone singing from her handbag. She looked at her display and her heart lurched. *Mason.* "Hello." Mason's soothing words greeted her.

"Clair, it's Mason. Um, I'm not sure if you remembered that I was coming around for you at nine. I'm here at your house, but you're not."

Clair gasped and slapped her forehead. "I'm so sorry." She'd been so caught up in her discussion with Christina and then Detective Anderson that she'd completely lost track of time. "Listen, I had to deal with something, or should I say someone, and it couldn't wait."

"I know, Charlotte filled me in. How did it go?" he asked.

She frowned. "Not very well, I'm afraid. But on the bright side, I did find out some interesting information from Detective Anderson."

"Oh." He paused as if contemplating what to say next. "Charlotte mentioned you needed to head into work. Instead of coming back home, what do you say I swing by Tea 4 Two, grab us a couple of fresh coffees and some pastries, then I'll meet you there and you can tell me all about it?"

Her cheeks warmed and his caring tone seeped through her veins. *He sounds like a concerned boyfriend.*

Clair cut her wayward thoughts short. He was there to help clear her name, not find a girlfriend. At least by the time he'd arrive, she'd have had a chance to change her sweaty shirt into one of the spares she kept in her office.

"Okay. I'll see you soon."

Chapter Seven

MASON'S BODY HUMMED with anticipation. He'd been looking forward to seeing Clair again, he just hadn't realised how much until he arrived at her house and she was nowhere in sight. His heart had skipped a beat when Charlotte informed him she was off chasing down a demon in the form of a tall blonde named Christina Jacobs. After the close call they'd had yesterday in Trent's office, he didn't want Clair taking any more chances with her life.

"Order for Mason." A husky voice called out across the café. He smiled at the tall, burly woman, grabbed his order and headed back to his car. The new owners of the Tea 4 Two Café had certainly turned it from the mediocre place it used to be into a hive of activity. It hadn't been the buzzing place to be when he'd lived in Ashton Point, although he'd very rarely ventured away from his computer. As a dorky, pimple-faced teenager, he hadn't socialised much with the locals. He was more interested in developing his computer programs and getting away from his father as soon as he was old enough.

Guilt tore at his heart. The promise his mother asked on her death bed flooded his mind. *Promise me, sweetheart...promise me you'll look after your father. It's going to be hard after I'm gone, but he's a good man and he loves you very much.*

Good man? Mason's gut twisted in knots and his heart hardened a little bit more. The love he had for his father had long since faded. Now, Mason was saddened at the time lost, the time his father dedicated to his business instead of his family.

Mason froze just as he was about to step out from the covered walkway to the carpark behind the cafe. The sinister tone of a man's words stopped him dead in his tracks.

"You better find out what James did with my money or maybe you'll follow in his footsteps and end up just like him. Dead."

End up just like him. Dead? Was his father's murderer within arm's reach? Mason's heart pummelled his chest. He quickly took cover in the alcove of the old candy bar doorway, out of sight of the two men. Thankfully it had been closed for some time. His ears were one hundred percent tuned to the conversation mere meters away.

The man's voice lowered an octave. "Listen, Mr Edwardson, this isn't the time or the place to discuss business."

The voices went silent and Mason, held his breath a moment, hoping they hadn't left. He spotted the retreating figure of Emmerson Bancroft heading towards her father's accounting office. Mason shook his head, wondering how she managed to still look the same as she had since primary school. Same bleached-blonde hair, same brown eyes. The only difference was she was now as tall as him. Mason's attention was quickly diverted back to the male voices, but now they seemed quieter than before. Careful not to be noticed, he leant as close to the edge of the walkway as he could, straining to hear.

"Listen, Gorson, I'm not leaving 'til I get some answers."

"You're right. James was my partner, but our partnership was very new and I've only been in town a short while. We didn't work on the same projects together. He didn't confide in me about your investment, but as far as I know, there is no money."

Partner? My dad had a business partner? He chanced a momentary glance in their direction. Thankfully, neither of them had seen him. He drew a blank. The faces of the two men didn't ring any bells. The short, stocky one with a bad 1960s oily comb-over, claiming to be the business partner, shuffled on his feet and a cold shiver skulked up Mason's spine. He had a gut feeling about this man and it wasn't pretty. He looked as shady as they come.

"I want my money back," Edwardson said in a demanding voice. "I don't care what you have to do to get it, but you will find my money, Mr Gorson, or so help me, I won't be held responsible for my actions."

Mr Gorson sighed and brushed his fingers through his greasy hair. "Let me have a look and see what I can find out. I can't promise anything but I will look into it for you. Like I said, we kept our projects separate. I figured out pretty quickly that James and I weren't exactly on the same page when it came to business. It wouldn't surprise me if James took your money for himself. I was contemplating dissolving the partnership just before he met his ill-fated demise."

Mr Edwardson scanned the carpark then turned to leave. "Just find my money. I'll expect a call from you in the next twenty-four hours. And I suggest you don't make me wait too long." He stormed off, leaving Gorson standing there alone.

Mason's chest started to burn. He hadn't realised he was holding his breath. Sucking in warm air, he waited until the coast was clear then made a beeline for his car, his pulse pounding in his head. "This just keeps getting better and better. First Stella, then Roland, now Gorson…who will it be next, Dad?"

He pulled up outside CC's Simply Cupcakes. The pink, chocolate-brown, and white frosted sign above the door and pale-pink window frames definitely suited a 1950s vibe. The place was a hive of activity. People lined up to grab the sweet treats. He glanced down at the bag of pastries in his hand and his stomach let out one loud grumble. "Why did I bother buying these, when I could feed my sweet tooth here?"

The inside matched the outside. Pink and chocolate brown stripe walls. Chalk menu boards, framed in gold, with cute detailed pictures of cupcakes strategically placed. Glass counter cabinets hosted some of the most amazing and intricate cupcake designs he'd ever seen. *Who knew cupcakes were so popular? Not me.*

His breath caught in his throat as Clair popped into view at the other end of the counter, talking and laughing with Suzi. Mason stood and watched her emerald-green eyes sparkle as she spoke. She was a vision of beauty. A sweet, delectable beauty, and way out of his league. After all, what woman would be interested in a geek who obsessed over computers 24/7?

Ignoring the twinge of hope deep in his gut, Mason threaded his way through the customers to where Clair was deep in conversation. He cleared his throat and she spun, gifting him with a smile that would rival any morning sunrise.

"I hope I'm not interrupting," he said as he placed the bag of pastries and two coffees on the counter.

She quickly ended her conversation. "Of course not."

The smell of frangipani and chocolate tickled his nose. He couldn't be sure if it was the shop or Clair, either way it smelt divine, and good enough to eat.

He gazed around the shop. "Wow, you sure are busy today. Is it like this all the time?"

"Most days. The pre-lunch rush has me run off my feet sometimes," she said, picking up a coffee. "But we've been really blessed. Charlotte and I worked our butts off in the first few years to build the business up. Well, Charlotte, mostly. Now we have great staff and a part-time pastry chef in the shop, which frees up Charlotte to work on the design side and special events, and me to branch out on my own with CC's Cupcake Haven."

"Like the Founder's Day Gala Dinner on Saturday night," he said.

She nodded then frowned. "How did you know about that?"

"Well, apart from it being the number one topic on the town's gossip train, I do remember the few I attended when I was younger. I also happened to see the poster on the wall in the café earlier."

"Oh, right. I suppose you could say that it's the most popular event this time of year. Everyone who's anyone is there and it gives us normal folk a chance to sport the formal attire for a night."

A pang of jealousy ricocheted through his body. As if she wouldn't already have a date for an event such as the gala dinner. He shook off the thoughts, knowing that if they didn't clear her name, she wouldn't be attending anything for the next twenty to life. The notion turned his blood to ice. "Is there a place we can talk?"

She paled. "Yes, this way."

He followed her through the kitchen and they entered a room that looked like an office. She turned and pointed toward an antique gold and burgundy chaise lounge in the corner. "Shall we sit?"

His back stiffened, but he nodded. "Sure."

"Okay, do you want to go first or shall I?" Clair asked.

Mason ignored his increasing heartrate. "Ladies first."

"Cool," Clair said as she flicked her leg underneath her and shuffled into a more comfortable position. "Turns out Christina was at the police station, so I confronted her about the article in the paper and things got a little heated."

"How heated?" he asked.

"Oh, nothing I couldn't handle, but enough to alert Detective Anderson. He came out and I thought what better way for Christina to print the truth than to hear the latest details first hand? Turns out the message we overheard in Trent's office was recorded the day before his murder, so that clears me, but also leaves the question. If it wasn't me he was meeting, who, then?"

"My bet is Stella," he said with confidence. "We know they knew each other. Anything else?"

Clair nodded. "They hadn't heard about their marriage so I'm sure Christina will have a field day with that bit of information. Both men were killed in a similar fashion, with a round object. On the night I found the body, I noticed a round object missing from the table near the entrance. It fits the description of the murder weapon and that means it most probably is the same killer. Turns out they searched your dad's offices and computers and came up empty, but they're interested in his mobile phone. They haven't been able to locate it. If we find his phone, we might find the missing piece of evidence to clear my name." Clair's face flushed. Mason watched her slender neck as she gulped down water from a drink bottle. "Your turn," she said.

"Just as I was leaving the Tea 4 Two Café, I happened to overhear a very interesting conversation between two locals."

"Do tell," Clair said eagerly swapping legs as she got comfortable.

Unable to keep the information under wraps, he blurted it, barely taking breaths between sentences. "Edwardson's threat sounds real to me."

Clair's brow furrowed. "I've only met Norman Gorson a few times and I don't really know Mr Edwardson or his wife that well. They moved into

town last year when they bought the Stewart Farm."
She paused. "Come to think of it, he has made some
pretty large acquisitions for the farm and I heard
Mavis Stevenson talking last week about his flash new
building plans. Some sort of housing extension on
the farm."

Mason couldn't shake the niggle in the base of
his neck. "What I don't get is why kill him, if he
wanted his money back? You can't get money from a
dead man. Like you said, we have more questions
than answers."

They sat in silence, mulling over his questions.
Clair had the cutest frown on her face that made him
smile.

"I've got it." Clair sprung off the couch and her
eyes sparkled as if a lightbulb had just turned on in
her head. "It's just an idea, but supposing Stella is
innocent and the phone message has nothing to do
with his death, what if Edwardson didn't mean to kill
him?"

"What? Like an accident?" Mason asked with
raised eyebrows.

"Not so much an accident, but an impulse retaliation that resulted in murder. A murder that Edwardson covered up and used me as the perfect scapegoat for. What if he went to see him to get his money back, and in a fit of rage lashed out and struck him down harder than he meant to?"

Pleased with her deductions, Clair smiled a disarming smile that had Mason's stomach turning inside out.

Why does she have to be so damn gorgeous?

"If what you say is true, why kill him at the Sweets mansion? Surely there'd be better ways of disposing of the body?"

She joined him again on the lounge, her excitement bubbling over. "Think about it, with our meeting scheduled at seven, I provided Edwardson with the perfect out. There are a number of ways he could have found out about our meeting. It was no secret. I've been so excited about finally closing the deal that I've been blabbing to everyone for the past month. James was always rushed for time, he probably had him meet him there for convenience. They argued and maybe in a rage—" she smacked her fist into her palm, "—wham, he slugs him one with the missing object."

Her words made some sense, but could it really be that easy.

"Finally, a solid lead," she squealed, throwing her arms around his neck.

His heart squeezed in his chest and he fell back on the chaise lounge, his arms fastening around her. They froze, gazes locked. The frangipani scent of her perfume tickled his nostrils and heat radiated from her body. Her cheeks glowed the warmest crimson blush. Clair bit her bottom lip and Mason suppressed a groan deep in his gut. Her lips were so close. Dare he kiss her? *What are you waiting for man? Do it.* He suddenly felt like a schoolboy, too shy to make the first move.

Too late.

"I'm so sorry," she said, pushing against his body to right herself. "I guess my excitement got the better of me."

He cleared his throat and pushed his glasses up on his nose with his right pointer. His body instantly regretted the loss of her touch. "No harm done," he said through a forced smile. "I'm glad we have a lead to follow, but we still need to find out the connection between Stella and Roland Trent in order to rule her out. Maybe we should get your name cleared before we start celebrating."

Clair ran her palms down her jeggings. "Of course," she said, avoiding his gaze. Bolting off the chair as if she'd sat on hot coals, she turned and grabbed her bag from the bottom draw in the filing cabinet and headed for the door. "No time like the present. The sooner we speak to Mr Edwardson, the sooner I can clear my name and you can get back to your life on the Gold Coast."

Mason's heart dropped. In the past few years it had been very clear that he didn't have room for a woman in his life, but the thought of going back home and not seeing Clair every day filled him with dread. She was a breath of fresh air, slowly seeping into every pore of his geek body. She may not be attracted to him, but that wouldn't stop him seeing her named cleared.

"Don't you think we should call Detective Anderson and tell him about Edwardson?" Mason asked as he followed suit.

She spun and her sharp gaze halted him mid-step. "This is our find. If it turns out I'm right, I'll happily serve him up on a platter to our dear Detective."

"Do you even know where he lives?" Mason asked.

"If I remember rightly, Charlotte did a one-off delivery for his wife a month or so ago, so we should still have the address on file."

There was obviously no changing her mind, so he didn't bother. "Shall I drive this time? I have my car out front."

"Why not?" He followed her into the bustling shop. "I just have to tie up a few loose ends before I leave. I'll be ten minutes, tops. Do you mind?"

"Not at all, I'll wait over by the door," he said. *The perfect place to watch you while you work.*

Chapter Eight

CLAIR JERKED HER head up from behind the counter and looked toward the exit. Mason stood leaning against the wall just inside the door, looking positively sinful. *How could I have got it so wrong?* A fresh wave of embarrassment worked its way up her neck to her cheeks. She pretended to check the order book, then counted the packets of icing sugar under the counter. Anything to give her a moment to recoup.

She had no idea what possessed her to throw her arms around his neck. The only way he could have been clearer about his intentions was if he had "not available" painted on his forehead for all to see. The constant pounding of her heart was enough to send her crazy.

Wouldn't be the first time she hadn't caught the eye of a man and it won't be the last. *So, he's not interested. I can deal with that.* She had stalled long enough. Clair quickly jotted down the Edwardson's address from the order book and shoved it in her pocket. Her eyes caught Suzi as she re-entered the main serving area. "Suzi, I'm off now. Charlotte will be in later to work on the cupcakes for the gala Saturday night."

Suzi's golden eyes lit up like yellow topaz glowing in the sunlight. "Oh, I can't wait 'til Saturday evening. It's going to be the best Founder's Day dinner ever."

"Really? Why's that?" Clair asked.

"Because for once I won't be attending alone. I'll have Daniel on my arm."

"Daniel? From *The Chronicle*?" Clair asked with raised eyebrows. The sheepish glint in Suzi's eyes answered her own question. "I had no idea you two were an item."

Suzi blushed. "We're not. At least not yet, but I'm working on it."

"Good for you." Suzi's happiness was like a lead boot tied to her heart. Clair chanced a glance in Mason's direction. *It's not like I'll have a date for the dinner. I won't have time anyway, I'll be focused on the cupcake display, or in jail.*

"Okay, I'm off. Enjoy the rest of your day and if you or Pierre need to use any of the supplies set aside for the weekend, can you make sure you write it up in the order book so I can replace it before Friday?"

"Sure thing. Bye," said Suzi, as she returned to serve the next customer.

"Bye." Clair headed toward the exit, her eyes narrowed and a new determination filled her with renewed energy. *I will not go down for these murders and there'll be no more male distractions.*

"Ready to go?" he asked as she approached.

"You betcha," she said as she walked straight past him toward his car, his jaw dropping in the process.

Mason moved faster than she had ever seen and was beside her in an instant. "Right, let's get this show on the road."

"Do you want to play good cop or bad cop?" she asked as Mason drove south toward the old Stewart farm.

"Excuse me?" he said in a questionable tone.

She rolled her eyes and sighed. "One of us has to play the baddy, I just wanted to get the game plan down before we get there."

"Clair, I don't think either of us should be playing the bad cop. He's not likely to give us any information if we storm in there demanding it. I think we need to be careful. If he's the murderer and realises we've worked it out, he might just decide to do something about it." Mason gripped the steering wheel harder as he turned down the semi-gravel road.

"All right, I see your point." She sighed and a brush of air escaped her lips. A frown marred Mason's face. *What is that all about?* She wondered. Tension settled in her stomach as they turned into Edwardson's driveway.

Mason continued. "I think the best angle would be an honest one, without throwing any accusations around. You're simply here to try and prove your innocence, not accuse him of murder."

"I guess you're right." She succumbed to his logical point of attack.

He turned off the engine and looked Clair square in the eyes. "The last thing we want is to become statistics. There are a lot of places to hide a body out here, so let's be careful."

No distractions, no distractions, no distractions, she chanted in her head as her chest tightened, lost in the spellbinding depths of his deep Mediterranean-blue eyes. *Focus.*

"I have an idea. Why don't I take the lead? I'll inform Mr Edwardson that I am looking into my father's clients in the prospect of taking over his business? That way, if he truly is looking for his money, he will relish in spilling his guts in the hopes I can find it. If he's our murderer… I guess we'll know soon enough."

Gorgeous and smart. He'll definitely make some woman very happy someday. A jolt of jealousy compounded the tightness in her chest. Forcing a smile, she said, "Good idea."

Clair's enthusiasm took a beating when their persistent knocks on Edwardson's door went unanswered. She'd almost given up when a hollow thump boomed from the side of the house.

"What was that?" Mason asked, his gaze shooting toward the source of the noise.

Clair shrugged. "I'm not sure, but it sounded like it was coming from the back yard," she said in a hesitant tone.

Clair shadowed Mason as he followed the continuous thumping. It pounded inside her head like the thunderous crack of someone hitting a snooker ball into a corner pocket, but twenty times louder. Her gaze caught a tall, stocky, shirtless man with shoulders the size of a boxer. He held an axe airborne as he brought it down in one swoop, splintering a stump of wood in two. She hadn't even realised Mason had stopped until she barrelled right into him, catching her before she fell on her backside.

"Are you okay?' he asked.

Her skin burned under his touch. She froze a moment, Mason's gaze hypnotising her. Clair opened her mouth but the words vaporised into thin air.

Holy cow, there he goes again, distracting me when I'm supposed to be concentrating on proving my innocence. And now I also have to contend with a semi-naked man, doing his best impersonation of a male model in a wood chopping contest?

No male distractions. She cleared her throat. "Yes, of course I'm all right. I just lost my footing on the uneven ground, that's all."

Liar.

"Oh." Mason paused as she fiddled with her shirt smoothing the imaginary creases out. He smirked. "I thought it might have had something to do with the sweaty, almost-naked man over by the barn."

Her eyes widened and a betraying blush flooded her cheeks. If only the ground would open up and swallow her whole. "Don't be ridiculous. I *have* seen men chop wood before, you know," she snapped.

"Half-naked men?" he pried.

Annoyance fuelled her reddened cheeks and she folded her arms across her chest. "Are we going to go and question Mr Edwardson, or stand here and debate the man's clothing or lack thereof?"

He held his hands up. "Okay, okay."

Clair pushed past Mason and headed toward the barn. As she neared the wood pile, she wondered what Mason's body would look like half-naked chopping wood. His broad, tanned shoulders glistening under the scorching Australian sun, sweat streaking down his chiselled abs.

For goodness sake, you'll be having those thoughts from jail if you don't stay focused. She blanked all images of men from her mind and sucked in a deep breath. Her focus returned to the man in front of her. The possible murderer.

Her back warmed, and she knew Mason was near. His presence reassured her. Maybe he was Superman in disguise. She could definitely do with some extra-terrestrial magic right about now.

Mr Edwardson turned, his darkened eyes glaring straight through her, and she felt uneasy in his presence.

"What do you want?" he barked.

She swallowed around the lump in her throat. "Mr Edwardson, it's Clair McCorrson, I'm not sure that we've been properly introduced but I was hoping I might be able to have a word with you about James Hapworth."

A sly smirk spread across his face. "Are you the McCorrson woman I have to thank for killing that deceitful, two-faced excuse for a man?"

Clair's stomach dropped. "No, I didn't kill James Hapworth." *Why does everyone think I could do such a horrible thing to another human being?* "But someone is trying to make it look like I did."

His back suddenly stiffened, his gaze firing daggers at her. "That's not my problem."

His words ignited the fire in her belly. "I think you have information that may help prove my innocence."

A chill skulked up her spine as he slowly moved toward them. Her body tensed and within seconds Mason was in front of her, shielding her from an advancing man that could break her in two without putting a hair out of place. She took a deep breath and made a conscious effort to push her fears aside.

Mason cleared his throat. "Mr Edwardson," he said, sticking his hand out mid-air. "My name is Mason Hapworth. James Hapworth was my father." Edwardson stopped, a frown creased his forehead. "We were hoping you had some information that can help piece together what happened in time to stop an innocent woman from going to prison for a crime she didn't commit."

He nodded and finally shook Mason's hand. "Kent Edwardson."

Without even realising it, her eyes dropped from Kent's eyes to the contoured lines of his chest.

Mason's lips thinned. "If it's not too much trouble, do you think you might consider putting a shirt on? Men's bare chests aren't really my thing."

"Oh, sorry, man. It doesn't take long to work up a sweat, especially with the sun so hot this time of day," he said as he covered up. "I'd like to say I'm sorry for your loss, but as far as I'm concerned, James Hapworth was as dirty as they come."

Clair eagerly side stepped around Mason. "Really? Why do you say that, Kent? It is okay if I call you Kent isn't it?" She asked, fluttering her eyelashes in his direction.

"Of course."

She glanced toward Mason and his blue eyes widened. A knot of frustration formed in her belly.

So, what if she had to flirt to get answers? She'd try almost anything to stay out of jail. *Almost.*

Mason continued. "Apart from helping Clair prove her innocence, I'm looking into his business affairs and not all is what it appears to be. What was the nature of your interactions with my father?"

Kent's expression darkened. "We made a business transaction together, but turns out he's a thief, or should I say *was* a thief. He stole a hundred and fifty grand from me. He gave me this big spiel about an investment in some apartments by the waterfront that were going to bring in millions for investors and I fell for it hook, line, and sinker."

Clair's brows knitted together. "Apartments?"

Kent huffed. "Apparently, it was hush-hush and he dished me some garbage about it being invitation only for the selected few."

"So, why the sudden change of heart?" Mason asked.

"My wife's father is ill. Cancer. We need the money for his treatment. The thing is, my wife doesn't know I gave it to him." Kent picked up pieces of chopped wood and started piling them by the fence. "I know it was a stupid thing to do."

"So, you're not building extensions out here?" Clair asked, disappointed that her information was incorrect.

Kent's hearty laugh filled the stilled air. "I hardly think so. Where on earth did you get a crazy idea like that?"

Clair frowned and embarrassment clawed at her chest. *That'll teach me to believe everything I hear.*

"So you asked my father for your money back?" Mason asked.

Kent threw another log on the pile. "Damn straight I did. Last week. He had the gall to feed me some bogus story about how the deal fell through and the money's vanished on the other end and it had nothing to do with him. More like he'd pocketed it for himself."

Clair pushed for answers. "So, you decided to take matters into your own hands and when you didn't get the answers you wanted, you flew into a fit of rage, you retaliated and James ended up dead."

"What?" Kent erupted in fits of laughter and the log of wood he held, thundered to the ground. "That is the most absurd thing I've ever heard. I didn't kill him. Oh, I wanted to, believe me, but I didn't."

Adrenaline coursed through her body. "Maybe you didn't mean to."

He shook his head. "You're wrong. Why would I kill him? I can't get my money from him if he's dead. Besides I wasn't even in town. I went to see my wife in the Blue Mountains. She's staying with her parents while her father has treatment. We both accompanied him for his first treatment and there are a number of people who can verify my presence, including the staff at Nepean Hospital. I only arrived home late last night."

Clair's body deflated as if she'd been hit in the gut with one of Kent's blocks of wood. *Now what?* Her gaze caught Mason's and he looked just as disappointed as she was.

"Do you know a man by the name of Roland Trent?" Mason asked.

Kent shook his head. "Nope, is that the other man they found murdered?"

Mason nodded. "Yes."

"If you want to point your finger at anyone," Kent said, as he continued to stack wood. "I'd be looking at that partner of his, Norman Gorson. He claims to not know anything about the deal. When I caught up with him to find out what happened to my money, he tried to tell me he had no idea what I was talking about. You can't tell me business partners don't talk."

Mason's brow creased. "I wasn't aware he had a partner."

Or a wife for that matter, Clair thought.

Kent huffed. "You and most of the town. If I had to guess who had the most to lose, it would be Norman. Maybe he killed him."

Clair's mind sped into overdrive as the cogs of information slotted together. *Maybe the woman he was meeting had something to do with this real estate deal.* James suckered people into investing in a bogus real estate scheme, and then stole their money. Norman found out James was embezzling money from the business, confronted him and killed him.

"Thank you for your time, Kent," she said, thrusting her hand in his direction. "We'll let you get back to your wood chopping."

He threaded his hardened calloused hand in hers and shook it. "You're welcome. Good luck. Hope you find the culprit before it's too late." He turned towards Mason and shook his hand. "I'd hate to see jail come between you two lovebirds."

Clair froze and she felt the blood drain from her face in spades. *Lovebirds?* She was about to correct him when the deep timbre of Mason's voice assaulted her ears.

"Oh, we're not together," Mason said as he sidestepped away from Clair. "I just don't believe in sending an innocent woman to prison for a crime she didn't commit."

His words crushed her heart, as did the sudden distance he put between them. *Gee, no need to sound so happy about it.* His actions and words confirming what she'd already suspected back in the shop. He wasn't interested in her.

Clair couldn't stomach one more second of this conversation. "Thanks again, Kent." Turning, she stalked toward the car, ignoring the call of her name as it blended with the shrilling rustle of the surrounding trees.

Chapter Nine

"WHAT IS WITH you these last few days?" Charlotte asked as she measured flour for the third batch of cupcakes. They'd both agreed to head into the shop early to get a head start on the preparations for tomorrow's gala dinner. "You've been a grumpy pain in my butt since Mason dropped you home the other day."

Why did Charlotte have to mention his name? Clair's stomach crunched, thinking of her silly adolescent behaviour the other day. She'd behaved like a school girl who had a crush on the nerdy star of the chess club. He made it clear he wasn't interested, otherwise why hadn't he kissed her when she'd absentmindedly thrown her arms around his neck?

"Well?" Charlotte barked.

Clair huffed and looked her square in the eyes. "Well, what?" Charlotte already thought her love life sucked, no use adding fuel to the fire.

"Don't ignore me like I'm not here," she said, adding one ingredient at a time to the bowl. "You know I'll just keep bugging you 'til I get the truth."

"All right, if you really want to know, I haven't been able to find the link between Stella and Roland Trent yet and I've been unable to contact Norman Gorson, James Hapworth's business partner, and I'm getting frustrated." Clair moved over to the doorway and peered into the shop. Suzi seemed to have things under control. *Great, no escape there.* "I've tried calling him several times and it goes straight to voicemail. I even went down to his office but it was locked."

Charlotte stopped stirring and narrowed her eyes at Clair. "I know, you've told me that already. There's something else. Has it anything to do with a handsome computer programmer from Surfers Paradise that hasn't visited the house since he dropped you off?" Charlotte said in an inquisitive tone.

Clair froze. She tried to squash the betraying blush that ran from her neck up to her cheeks but failed miserably.

"Ah ha, I was right. It does have something to do with Mason." Charlotte pushed the bowl aside, grabbed Clair's hand and dragged her on to the couch in the office. "Out with it."

"Charlotte, please, we have too much to do," Clair said hoping for a distraction.

"Pfft," Charlotte said as she flicked her hand over her shoulder. "It can wait. Since we came in today, we're ahead of schedule anyway."

Her pulse sped up and her body tensed. Clair's nose twitched remembering Mason's strong scent. She was sitting in the exact spot Mason sat only days ago.

"Spill," Charlotte repeated. "You know I'm a great listener."

Clair knew her sister was the queen of persistence. "It's nothing, really. I accidentally, maybe slightly subconsciously threw myself at Mason the other day. Actually, right here, and he couldn't get away from me quick enough."

Charlotte pulled back, her eyebrows raised. "Excuse me?"

Clair's heart jolted. "It's no big deal."

"Wait, wait, wait just a minute." Charlotte's flushed expression would have made her laugh if it weren't because of the dismal state of her love life. "I'm a little confused. I think you better explain it from the beginning."

She looked up at Charlotte's sapphire-blue eyes. They were laced with concern, and it gutted her to know her sister worried about her. Clair flashed a comforting smile. "I'm okay, really. Mason was here in the office the other day to tell me about the conversation he overheard between Gorson and Kent Edwardson. I may have gotten a tad excited. We were sitting here on the couch when he'd told me what he heard and between the good news and him smelling so intoxicatingly good, and sitting so close to me, I kind of threw my arms around his neck and I somehow ended up lying on top of him."

Charlotte's jaw dropped.

Embarrassment bled through her body and she grabbed Charlotte's hands in hers. "It was the perfect moment to kiss me, and I did want to kiss him. His soft lips were inches from mine, all I had to do was lean in, but he looked alarmed more than anything and I knew I'd made a huge mistake."

Charlotte sat still, her gaze drilling into Clair.

"Say something. Anything, please," Clair pleaded.

"I cannot believe a sister of mine waited this long to confide in me," Charlotte said, her words laced with hurt. "Why didn't you tell me?"

Clair dropped her chin down. "Why do you think? I was embarrassed. I like him. I like him a lot and I thought he may have felt the same, even just a little bit. He's been amazing with the way he's helped me out this past week. Anyway, the last thing I should be thinking about is kissing Mason when my freedom hangs in the balance."

"Sweetie, just because he didn't kiss you doesn't mean he doesn't like you," Charlotte said.

Clair stood, her nerves almost ready to jump out of her skin. "I really don't want to talk about it anymore."

"Have you considered that he might be just as nervous as you are? After all, he could have been waiting for you to make the first move."

Her eyes widened. *Me? Make the first move?* She flopped back on the couch, her heart deflating like a busted beach ball. "Do you think so?"

The corner of Charlotte's lip turned up. "Yes, I do. I haven't spent a lot of time with him, but from what I can gather he seems shy and reserved. A computer programmer who has spent more time with his computer than with any real women. Remember how he has the Clark Kent look going on?"

Clair nodded.

"Maybe he has the disguise side worked out perfectly, but what if the real man underneath has never really ventured out of his comfort zone?" Charlotte asked, brushing a stray piece of hair behind her ear. "I think there's something there and I don't think you should give up."

"Really?"

"Really. In fact, I think you should take the first move and ask him to go to the Gala dinner with you tomorrow night. What harm could it do? And I'm sure you really don't want to rock up alone."

Definitely not. The memory of Mason's arms around her caused a cascade of tingles to flutter in her belly. In the past, she'd been in relationships where the man took the initiative. Maybe it was time to turn the tables. "Perhaps you're right. I'll think about it. Right now, I think the best thing for me to do is head back over to see if I can catch Norman Gorson. I'll camp outside his office until he returns if I have to."

"Do you think it's wise to go alone?" Charlotte asked, concern filled her eyes. "Maybe you should call Mason. He could go with you, just in case."

The thought of seeing Mason again had her insides squirming. Half in excitement and half in dread. "Maybe you're right. Maybe I'll call him on the way. Are you sure you'll be all right here without me?" Clair asked as she squeezed her sister.

"Of course, now on your way," Charlotte said pulling Clair up off the lounge as she stood.

"Thanks for listening. Anyone ever tell you you're the best sister in the world?"

Charlotte swished her wavy red locks from side to side and grinned sheepishly. "Of course I'm the best sister in the world, but don't let Cassidy hear you say that." Clair burst out laughing and Charlotte joined her. They linked arms and headed out to the workshop once more.

"When is that sister of ours coming home anyway?" Charlotte asked.

"I spoke to her last week and I'm pretty sure she said she was extending her stay for another few weeks. So that would make it next week sometime, I suppose." Clair missed her other sister terribly. She gave Charlotte one more hug, then grabbed her bag and headed for the door. "I'd better go, if I want to greet Cassidy wearing my clothes instead of prison-issue green."

Clair's call to Mason went straight to the message bank. "At least I called him. Not my fault he didn't answer," Clair muttered to herself as she pulled up outside Norman Gorson's office. A sliver of excitement erupted in her belly when she saw his door slightly open. *Thank goodness.* By the time she reached the door her heart was pounding in her head.

"Hello," she said as she slowly pushed the door open. "Mr Gorson, my name is Clair McCorrson."

She scanned the empty office, her gaze catching the large photograph on the wall above the reception counter of a man that looked like he was stuck in the 1970s. Gorson's name was engraved in bold lettering underneath.

Silence.

"Great, he's not here?" *So why is the door ajar?* There was no use hanging around an empty office. Turning to leave, her heart lurched at the sudden mumble coming from a back office.

"Mr Gorson?" she called again, looking toward the direction of the noise. A tingle shot up her spine as the voice became louder. *Finally, I might get some answers.*

Refusing to miss the opportunity, Clair stepped forward, her hand poised to push the door open and her breath caught in her throat.

"Don't you dare hang up on me, or I swear your life won't be worth living. You promised me no-one would be able to trace it back to me."

Holy cow. Is that Norman Gorson's voice? What does he mean by, "your life won't be worth living?"

"We had a deal. You help me make arrangements and I make you a very rich man. I'm so close to getting out of this hick town, and neither you, nor James' death is going to stop me. And don't call me Normy."

Clair's hand shot to her mouth to muffle her startled gasp. *Arrange what? A murder?*

This was pure gold. She couldn't believe her luck but it would all be for nothing if she got caught spying. A tall, fake potted palm to the side of the door caught her eye. *Perfect.* Obtrusive enough to hide behind, while still giving her a clear view of the office through the glass window.

"I told you I don't care how you do it. Just do it." He paused, listening. Clearly frustrated, Mr Gorson paced the office, his appearance was a little worse for wear compared to the picture above the reception desk. Sweat beaded his forehead and Clair's stomach revolted at the enormous sweat patches under his armpits. *Gross.*

"Do what?" she whispered.

His arm flew in all directions, waving left and right. His face grew the brightest shade of crimson-red she'd ever seen, like a beetroot and it looked like he was about to burst a blood vessel.

"Stop saying that. They can't be empty. The money should be there. You said it was all set and there would be no hiccups," he snapped.

Her spine straightened and her brow creased. *Money, what money? Did he mean Mr Edwardson's money?* Why would Mr Gorson have it, if he'd paid it to James?

The information swirled inside her mind like a whirlpool out of control finally coming to the only conclusion possible. *Gorson stole it.*

Mr Gorson embezzled the company's money, including that of James' that's why when he ran into Mr Edwardson this morning he said there was no money because there is *no money.* The question was, did James know, and if he did, was it his undoing?

Her jaw dropped, stunned by her clever deductions.

"You better find it, or else. By this time next week, I should be sunbaking on a beach on the other side of the world. If you can't find the money there will be hell to pay. Do we understand each other?" He slammed down the phone and fell back into his chair.

Clair swayed on her feet. The stuffy corner she'd hidden in suddenly closed in around her, suffocating her. Combined with information overload and the overwhelming musky scent and heat in the office, it was like being wrapped in a wool blanket on a hot summer day.

She wanted to storm in there and demand answers, but her feet wouldn't move. If he did kill James, what would stop him from killing her right now? There would be no witnesses. Charlotte was the only one who knew she was coming here, and what good would that do? All he had to do was hide her body and claim she never arrived.

Fear skulked up her spine. Her brain sent messages to her legs to get out, but her legs didn't seem to be receiving them. She squeezed her eyes shut and prayed she held it together. A sharp clicking sound from the desk snapped her eyes open. Mr

Gorson threw manila folders into his briefcase and snapped it shut. He was leaving.

Time had run out. It was get out or get caught. Adrenaline coursed through her veins as she silently bolted for the front door, careful not to alert him to her presence. Clair's heart sank, just as she closed the door behind her. She heard Mr Gorson's office door slam. *Did he see me?*

The illuminated flashing sign of the chemist next door caught her attention and she darted inside out of line of sight, she closed her eyes and rubbed her hand over her forehead, relieved the ordeal was over.

"Is everything all right, Clair?" A petite woman with a twangy voice asked.

Clair gasped and looked up. "Mary-Jane, I didn't see you there. Yes, everything's fine, I've a headache that's all and I've run out of painkillers." Clair wasn't about to tell her the truth. She felt like Pinocchio for lying, her nose growing longer by the second.

"You've come to the right place," she said as she walked toward the counter. "You take Panadol, if I'm not mistaken."

"Yes, that's right," she said.

Clair paid and grabbed the bag. She wasn't really lying, she did feel a headache coming on. Who could blame her? With no time to waste, she dialled Mason's number, eager to find out where he's been and fill him in on her findings.

Chapter Ten

"WHAT POSSESSED YOU to go there alone in the first place?" Mason asked as he placed one of his father's boxes on the kitchen table. "If you'd been caught, goodness knows what he might have done."

Mason had been sorting his father's possessions, hoping to locate his mobile phone when she rang. He insisted on her coming straight over, but now that she was receiving the third degree, she wished she hadn't. "I'm not completely hopeless, you know. I can take care of myself."

The hurt expression on his face gutted her.

"That's not what I meant," he said with a sigh.

"I did try and call you so you could come with me, but it went straight to message bank." She ignored the flip-flop of her stomach when he leaned in and placed his hand over hers.

"Sorry about that, I had some work calls that I needed to make, but if I'd known you were in danger..." He paused, pursing his lips together. "I just want you to be careful. It would destroy me if anything happened to you."

It would? The warmth of his hand blended into hers and she felt herself start to overheat. Her mind snapped back to reality. *He's just helping you out, nothing more. He doesn't like you that way, remember.*

She slipped her hand from his and pretended to sort through a stack of papers scattered on the table. Changing the subject, she asked, "So what is all this stuff anyway?" She noticed he pulled his chair closer to her before sitting down causing a cascade of tingles to flutter in her lower belly.

"My father's documents. Stella's out of town tonight visiting her sister in Budgewoi, so I thought I'd get a head start sorting this stuff and hopefully get lucky in finding his missing phone."

"Want some help?" Her lips blurted before she had a chance to put her mind into gear. The spicy scent of his aftershave teased her nostrils and she hadn't realised how much she wanted his answer to be yes.

He smiled and her heart somersaulted. Again. "I'd love some, but I insist that you stay for dinner as my guest. It's frozen pizza night, nothing flash, but it's the least I can do."

She nodded. "Well, I do have to eat and it would save me cooking when I get home."

"Perfect," he said as he placed a box in front of her on the table. "You can start here."

Her eyes widened. "What exactly am I looking for?"

"His phone for starters, but anything incriminating, I guess. I have no intention of following in dear, old Dad's footsteps. For all I care, Stella can have the business, but I am hoping to find something that will point us in the right direction to help find the real murderer."

They sat in a comfortable silence, sifting through box after box, sorting each into one pile or another. Clair closed her eyes a moment and rolled her neck in a circle to work out the kink that had developed over the past hour.

Mason frowned. "Are you okay?"

"Sure," she said as she placed another piece of paper on a pile.

His head turned toward the kitchen and a sharp gasp filled the room. "Oh, my goodness, it's seven o'clock. I can't believe how the time has flown by. I promised you dinner," he said, shooting into the kitchen.

"Mason, it's fine. I'm okay, really."

"Nonsense," he grumbled. "What sort of host would I be if I didn't serve my guest dinner as promised?"

"A preoccupied one." A giggle erupted from her belly at the sight of Mason flitting around the kitchen. "Do you have any idea how crazy you look right now?"

He paused, resting his hip against the kitchen bench, his soulful, apologetic eyes looking straight at her. "I guess I do look pretty silly, running around like a madman."

Clair smiled. "It will only take twenty minutes to cook, so pop it in the oven. That will give us twenty more minutes to keep working and then we'll take a well-earned dinner break. What do you say?"

His beaming smile ricocheted right through her body. "Smart and beautiful, how did I get so lucky." Mason froze, clearly stunned by his own words.

What the? Confusion embedded itself in the base of her stomach. He is either really polite or she'd totally misread the incident in her office the other day. He was like a yo-yo, playing catch me if you can with her heart.

No distractions, no distractions. The drawn-out silence bumped up the tension between them a notch. She huffed and brushed her hand in a dismissive action. "I bet you say that to all the girls." She quickly returned to sorting papers.

"Yeah, right, all the girls," he said in a flippant tone.

Clair's insides churned. She quickly changed the subject. "So, what's it like living in Surfers Paradise?" she asked.

He shrugged and joined her at the table. "Okay, I guess."

Okay, I guess? She paused, a frown marred her expression. "You guess? Isn't it supposed to be this fast-paced, exciting city that never sleeps? Lots of parties, women, that sort of thing."

He pushed his glasses up on the bridge of his nose and her chest clenched as the cutest blush covered the base of his neck. "I wouldn't know, I'm not really into that sort of stuff."

"What sort of stuff are you into?"

"My work, computer programming. It takes up pretty much most of my time. " He paused picking up a handful of documents from a box on the floor. "And you. What are you into?"

"Me?" she said with a raised eyebrow.

"Yeah, you," he said catching her focus. "Why are you so surprised?"

Clair found herself mesmerised by his inviting blue eyes. "Um..."

"I really like spending time with you. You're easy to talk to and in my world that's a rare find."

He does like me. She wanted to jump up and do a happy dance.

He continued. "Most of the women in Surfers are just out for a good time, it's great to meet a nice woman who can hold a conversation that isn't just focused on her looks or computers."

Nice? Now I'm nice?

Clair's stomach dropped. Her head was about to explode with his constant chopping and changing views. *And they say women are hard to read.* If only she could stay focused on proving her innocence, instead of being side-tracked by the gorgeous man sitting beside her. She sighed and picked up another document. Her eyes widened, and it was as if the words jumped right off the page and into her brain. She shot out of her chair, her heart pounding.

"I found something." She looked up barely able to believe her luck. "Incriminating evidence, I think."

Mason stood and was beside her in an instant. "What are you talking about?"

"It's right here on this piece of paper," she said as she handed it over. "A life insurance policy on your father."

"What?"

"For three million dollars and look who's the beneficiary," she said pointing, to the name at the bottom of the page.

Mason's eyes widened. "His grieving widow." Her hand shook as she handed the document to Mason. The corner of his lip turned up into a cheeky grin. "And taken out only two weeks before his death. Look who else's signature is here," he said pointing to the bottom of the page.

Clair's jaw dropped. "Roland Trent. I guess now we know the connection between them. The empty file in his office was obviously connected to this policy and maybe their marriage."

"Seems step-mother dear has a lot of explaining to do."

"Surely that's a motive for murder. Maybe Stella bumped him off for the money?" Clair asked, relief coursing through her system.

"It all comes down to money. Murder for money. From what you overheard in Mr Gorson's office and now this. Both have a motive for murder, but the question is, which one actually did the deed?" Mason said.

"Either way, I think we should tell Detective Anderson. If this is a secret Stella has been keeping, goodness knows what else she's hiding?"

His grin turned into an enormous smile that lit up the entire kitchen. "Definitely. You did it, Clair," he said picking her up and swinging her around, her legs dangling above the floor.

Clair gasped, her heart pitching into her throat. She gripped his broad shoulders as her body melded to his muscular frame. Her heart wanted more than just his arms around her, but her head knew it was just his reaction to her find. The oven buzzer pierced the air. *Saved by the bell.*

Reality crashed through her moment of euphoria as Mason set her down. They stood staring at each other, a comfortable silence between them. Her pulse raced. "That would be the pizza," she said with a smile.

"Yes, of course," he said bolting into action.

Great. There I was, standing arm in arm with a gorgeous guy and I have to go and spoil it by mentioning food. Why couldn't she have Charlotte's get-up-and-go confidence when it came to men? Charlotte's words rang out in her mind.

Maybe he has the disguise side worked out perfectly, but what if the real man underneath has never really ventured out of his comfort zone. I think there's something there and I don't think you should give up. I think you should take the first move and ask him to go to the Gala dinner with you tomorrow night. What harm could it do?

She watched him slice up the pizza, dividing it onto two plates. Clair ignored the butterfly chaos in her stomach, sucked in a deep breath and took a chance. "I don't suppose you're free tomorrow night?"

Mason paused, two plates held mid-air. "Tomorrow night?" he said, his eyebrows raised. "Isn't tomorrow night the Gala dinner?" he asked placing a plate for her at the table.

She nodded. "Yes, I was wondering if you had nothing better to do, I thought maybe you might want to go with me."

"Like a date?" he asked.

A date? I wish. "Well, like a business date. I figured most of Ashton Point will be in attendance, so it would be the perfect time to suss out Stella and also keep an eye on the town folk for any suspicious behaviour."

"I see," he said, taking a bite of his pizza.

You see what? She thought.

"You're right, it would be perfect timing to confront Stella about the insurance policy. It will be hard for her to deny or lie about it in front of witnesses." He paused as if contemplating her request. "On one condition?" he said.

Mason shuffled in his seat and she could have sworn she saw a trickle of sweat across his brow. Clair felt her stomach drop. "What condition?"

He bit his bottom lip. "You go out on a real date with me after this is all over."

Her knees jellied up and her jaw nearly hit the floor. "You want to go out on a date…with me?" she said flabbergasted.

He sat back in his chair and sighed, his eyes focused on the pizza on his plate. "I know I'm not like the usual guys you probably have knocking down your door, but I'd really like to go out on a proper date with you."

"You would?" Clair sat stunned. He nodded and the pain in his eyes crushed Clair's heart.

"Dating doesn't exactly come easy to me. I mean, I've had a few girlfriends but I've never felt as comfortable with them as I have with you. I enjoy your company, and you and I seem to be able to talk easily, which has never happened to me before. If I'm going to be honest, I really like you."

Clair's stomach felt like the butterflies had hatched inside as she sat, soaking up Mason's words. "I thought you didn't like me?"

His brow creased and his gaze caught hers. "What on earth gave you that idea?"

A crimson blush warmed her cheeks and she shrugged. "The other day when I got a little overexcited at the shop and threw my arms around your neck, it looked like you couldn't get away from me fast enough, so I figured I'd overstepped the mark." She frowned as he chuckled at her words.

"Are you serious? I wanted to keep my arms tight around you and tell you how I was feeling, but I wasn't sure if that was appropriate or not and the last thing you need right now is a distraction."

A distraction like Mason was *exactly* what she didn't need at the moment, but also what she desperately wanted. *Charlotte was right. I should learn to trust my sister's instincts.*

"Mason, listen—"

Before she could finish, Mason snapped up her empty plate and began scraping her pizza crusts into the bin. "It okay, Clair, I totally understand. I was way out of line."

"Mason?"

He continued. "I did say that I wasn't very good at this dating thing."

Mason?" she said louder in an effort to cut through the barrier he'd erected.

He continued stacking the dishwasher, oblivious to her voice. "I understand, I do. It's okay. I shouldn't have said anything. I promise once I help prove your innocence, I'll be out of your hair for good."

Frustration seeped through her entire body. "Mason," she yelled and he spun, jolted by her high-pitched voice. "Stop talking."

Mason's eyes widened and his jaw dropped, obviously stunned by her outburst.

Her heartrate kicked into overdrive but she couldn't hold back the giggle that smouldered in her belly. "I'd love to go on a real date with you, in fact, I wouldn't have minded your arms holding me tight the other day."

"Are you saying what I think you're saying?" Mason asked in a stunned tone.

Clair's mouth was too dry to speak, so she simply nodded. They stood in silence, their eyes locked on each other's while the electric tension between them soared. Two little words repeated in her head like clanging church bells. *No distractions.*

Clair felt a tug in her gut. "I like you, Mason, but I have to focus on finding the killer before I can think about dating anyone."

"I totally agree and you have my complete assistance," he said as he moved closer.

Clair fought the urge to throw her arms around him and kiss his lush lips. She knew if she got one taste of him she'd never want to stop. "So, is that a yes for tomorrow night?"

He brushed the stray strands of her tousled hair away from her face and smiled. "You've got yourself a date, and I guarantee I'll be the envy of every man in the room."

Chapter Eleven

NERVOUS ENERGY HAD Clair on her toes most of the morning. The day had been choc-a-block full of errands to complete before tonight's big event. Thankfully, they were closing the shop early, hoping to avoid any drama getting the cupcakes finished and over to the Ashton Point Resort in time to get back home and get dolled up for the evening.

"Are you okay delivering the last of the cupcakes?" Clair asked Charlotte as she flicked the sign on CC's Simply Cupcakes to closed and locked the door behind her.

"As long as you pick up my dress from Kelly at Snip 'n' Sew, I'll be fine." Charlotte said heading toward her car.

"Will do. Now go and I'll see you at home." Clair smiled and waved as Charlotte took off down the street.

She chuckled to herself. "Who doesn't decide what dress they're wearing to a formal dinner 'til the day before?" *Charlotte, that's who.* Clair shook her head, she couldn't believe how accommodating Kelly had been when Charlotte rushed her dress in to have it altered at the last minute.

Covered in a sheer line of plastic, Clair hung Charlotte's pristine cobalt-blue, sequined strapless dress over her arm as she exited Snip 'n' Sew. Her sister always liked to add a little sparkle to her outfits, and this evening was no exception. Whereas Clair had high hopes for Mason's approval with the fitted sleeveless, floor-length black-velvet gown she'd chosen for the night. It was plain, but elegant with a slit to the thigh on one side and accentuated with pearls, it was sure to get a reaction.

"Where are you, keys? I know you're in here somewhere," she muttered, searching her bag for her car keys, oblivious to the growing excitement around her.

Thwack.

"Watch where you're going, will you?" The woman's gruff voice snapped as Clair juggled Charlotte's dress and her bag, praying neither would end up on the filthy pavement.

"Excuse me?" Clair said, regaining her stability. *The nerve of the woman blaming me for what was clearly her fault.*

"Oh, it's you." Stella's sarcastic tone rang out.

Clair's blood began to boil at the sight of a smug Stella. The discovery of her deceit last night flooded her mind. "Sorry, Stella. I didn't see you there. I was just picking up Charlotte's dress for this evening. It's exciting, don't you think?"

Stella's lips thinned and she shrugged.

"You are going to the Founder's Day Gala dinner this evening, aren't you?" Clair asked. *Because Mason would love to chat with you.*

Stella paled and shook her head. "No, I don't think I can make it anymore."

"What…why not?"

"I really don't see what concern that is of yours, but if you must know, I've been under the weather the last few days and the doctor has advised me against going out at night." Stella pushed her handbag up on her shoulder and turned to leave.

Liar. Clair saw red and her mouth ran away from her before she could stop it. "How interesting.

I guess lying comes naturally to you. We both know you haven't been sick, unless you were lying to Mason about visiting your sister last night. You even lied to him about knowing Roland Trent."

Stella froze and slowly turned. A triumphant thrill ran up Clair's spine.

"I don't know what you're talking about," she said, her face suddenly drawn with age.

"Really?" Clair said hiking the dress up in her arms. "So lying, deceit, and murder were all part of your plan?"

Mortification clouded Stella's eyes. "Murder?" She gasped. "I had nothing to do with James' murder or Roland Trent's. I barely knew the guy."

"Ah huh, but you *did* know him," Clair said shaking her finger at her. Mrs Stevenson was right.

Stella sighed in resignation. "All right, all right, yes I met him through James. He was a business associate of his, that's all."

"So, it doesn't bother you that his name is signed on the bottom of James' life insurance policy next to yours, citing you as the beneficiary?"

Stella gasped and her mouth made a round O. "What insurance policy?"

"Oh, please, like you don't know. The one that states that his wife gets three million dollars in the event of his death. Conveniently signed by your lawyer, Roland Trent, who cannot be questioned. If they proved you murdered James for the money and Roland to keep your secret, the policy would be null and void. The police have it, so I'm sure they're going to want to chat with you very soon."

Stella paled, shock plastered over her face. "No, you've got it all wrong," Stella said suddenly, her sincere tone throwing Clair off kilter.

Clair's brows drew together and she stared intently at the woman. "You might not be attending the dinner tonight, but I suggest you stick around town."

Stella's sudden change in demeanour caught Clair off guard. Pain. Fear. Clair couldn't tell which one until Stella all but crumbled in front of her. Alarm rippled over her as tears gathered in Stella's eyes.

"Okay, you win," Stella said between sobs. "I've lied to Mason about a lot of things, including that silly curse stuff in the paper, but not about the murder. I could never kill James. Whether you believe me or not, I loved him, but I wasn't his wife. At least not officially."

What the... Clair's heart was about to jump right out of her chest.

"What exactly do you mean 'officially'?" Clair asked.

"I mean we've been living together on and off for the last twelve months and we loved each other, but he refused to get married. Something about how he'd already married the love of his life. I knew I'd get nothing and it would all go to Mason. After all the time I gave him, I'd walk away empty handed. I panicked. The policy is real, but I covered Mason's name and forged my name. I knew they'd question Roland Trent about it so I went to see him, to tell him to keep quiet. He refused, until I offered him half the money. To complete the whole charade, he arranged to have a new policy made, citing me as the sole beneficiary and had a marriage certificate forged."

Stunned, Clair stood and listened. *It was like she was living in her very own soap opera.*

Stella continued between garbled gasps. "But nothing is worth putting my life in danger, not even for James."

Clair frowned. "Danger? What are you talking about?"

"I did visit my sister last night and when I got back this morning, Mason's car wasn't in the driveway. So, I figured he was still at his mate's place or out doing whatever young men do these days and I wouldn't have to see him. When I walked through the front door, I got the biggest shock of my life. The place was like a war zone. Someone had ripped it apart. Cushions slashed to smithereens, pictures smashed, and cupboard and drawers flung open with the contents strewn all over the floor."

Clair's entire body stiffened. Stella's words hit her where she lived. *What if they'd come last night when she and Mason were there?* A cold shiver ran down her spine.

"I've no idea what they were looking for, but judging by the state they left it in, they didn't find it. I'm sorry, honey, but I'm not waiting around to see if they come back. For all I know, they'll think I have what they're looking for and come after me next."

The phone? Could it be James' phone they were looking for?

"Think, Stella, think hard. Do you know what they were looking for? Did James mention anything to you, show you something maybe?" Clair asked eagerly.

She shook her head. "No and I'm telling you the truth. We rarely talked about his work, especially lately. He was more secretive than normal." Stella checked the time on her phone. "I've told you all I know, now if you'll excuse me my sister is expecting me back today."

****

Clair threaded her mother-of-pearl earrings through her earlobes, the final addition to her outfit. Her stomach had been in knots all day, even after she'd fed the information about the break-in at Stella's back to Mason. He'd promised to call in and see Detective Anderson before heading back to his mate's place to get ready, which just made her worry more. A knock at her bedroom door startled her.

"Are you almost ready in there? Liam's here to pick me up and I want to see your dress before I go." Charlotte's voice called from the hallway.

Clair took one last glance at herself in the mirror and smiled. Her dress fitted snuggly to her figure and with the pearl choker and her unruly red locks secured in a French roll, she really did feel like a princess heading to her ball.

Satisfied with her appearance, she took a deep breath and opened the door. "Wow, Charlotte, you look amazing," Clair said, her heart warming as she leant in for a hug. She was blown away by Charlotte's dress and the way it hugged each of her curves. "You don't scrub up too bad."

They both giggled.

Charlotte stepped back and her glittered gaze washed over Clair. "It seems I get it all from you, sis. You look absolutely stunning. Mason is not going to know what hit him when you open that door tonight."

Clair blushed. "I hope so."

"He won't be able to take his eyes off you. You look like Audrey Hepburn from *Breakfast at Tiffany's*, but with red hair."

Clair burst out laughing. "Don't be silly, I do not." *Do I?*

She turned to look at her reflection one more time, twisting the stray ringlets around her face. "Do you really think I look like Audrey Hepburn?" she asked, a nervous energy shooting through her veins.

"Better," Charlotte said giving Clair a goodbye kiss on the cheek. "Liam and I will meet you there."

"Okay." Butterflies welled around in her stomach as Charlotte left her alone with her frayed nerves. It felt like she hadn't eaten in a week. Every time a glimmer of hope seeped into her heart, it was squashed just as quickly by the darkened cloud hanging over her future.

Two little words beat inside her head like a timpani drum. *No distractions.* She'd do well to keep that in mind this evening. The shrill of the doorbell made her jump.

Here goes.

Chapter Twelve

MASON PACED CLAIR'S steps, his heart running its own race inside his chest. He couldn't believe he made it in time, after the dreadful day he'd had. It was bad enough that he couldn't hire a suit, he had to buy one, and then he spent most of the afternoon with the police, dealing with the break-in at his father's house. He'd fed the information about Stella to Detective Anderson, but he didn't know what good it would do. Anderson was no closer to finding the murderer than he had been the night it happened. *What will it take, another murder before they realise they're wasting time?*

He rang the doorbell and waited. A cold shiver ran up his spine. *What if they had tried to break in when he and Clair were there?* She could have been seriously hurt or killed. Fear simmered and boiled up in Mason's throat at the thought. He wasn't trained in martial arts, but he'd sparred enough at the gym to defend himself. He knew in his heart that he would have and will do anything to protect Clair. She'd wormed her way into his closed heart and now he couldn't imagine not seeing her warm smile.

The door swung open and all the air escaped his lungs in one big whoosh. Clair was a picture of pure beauty. "Oh...my," he said, barely able to string two words together. Her emerald-green eyes sparkled under the burnt orange haze from the evening sunset. She did a little twirl and his heart skipped a beat.

Her eyes widened. "Where are your glasses?"

"Contacts," he said, pointing to his eyes. "Do you mind?"

"Mind? Not at all." Clair nodded toward her outfit. "You like?" she asked.

The shy glow in her cheeks almost matched the colour of her hair. "What's not to like?" It was going to be harder to keep focused tonight then he thought. "You look amazing." He held his hand out waiting for her touch.

"Thank you," she said, threading her hand in his.

His heart seemed to have overridden his brain and he pulled her close to within an inch of his electrified body. She gasped and her lips opened. He could feel the heat from her hand seeping through his. He prayed she didn't scold him for what he was about to do. He leaned in and his lips met hers.

The feel of her lips against his sent quivers of pleasure shooting through his body. She met his lips eagerly, her arms snaking around his neck. He knew he should have waited, but he couldn't help it. He'd never met another woman that made him feel so alive. After the real murderer was caught, he planned to stick around, if she'd let him. Which meant their attention tonight had to be on the dinner guests, not each other.

Reluctantly, he pulled away. Looking at her under the glow of the sunset, his heart somersaulted in his chest at how beautiful she was. He fought the urge to pull her close and kiss her again. "I'm sorry, but you just looked so beautiful."

Clair placed a soft finger over his lips. "It's quite all right. One kiss won't hurt and I'm hoping there might be some more when this is all over."

He smiled. "It's a promise," he said, holding his elbow out. "Now, how about we head to this shindig?"

Clair pulled the door closed behind her and threaded her arm in his. He looked down at the grey pin-striped, three-piece suit as they headed toward his car. "I feel a tad underdressed next to you."

"Seriously? I happen to think you look like a million dollars," she said with a beaming smile. "Don't forget to keep your eyes and ears open for anyone acting suspicious. Most of the town will be there, so if people are going to gossip, it will be tonight."

Clair sat down on the chair in the ladies' restroom, placing her black handbag beside her on the chair. She flicked her shoes off, exhaustion settling in every inch of her body. Since Stella was no longer a viable suspect, she'd hoped to corner Norman Gorson this evening, but that notion was instantly shot down since he hadn't arrived.

She'd smiled, greeted, eaten and even danced the night away and still, she was no closer to finding the murderer. Of course, Mason had been a hit with the women in town, even the married ones.

Clair's body tensed. *It's those glasses or lack thereof.* The women in town finally saw what she'd seen from the beginning and she didn't like it one bit. Realisation hit her like a cement truck. She was jealous. Her mother had always called jealously the "green-eyed monster" because it brought out the worst in people, and she was right.

Clair scolded herself. Mason had done nothing to sway her belief in him.

A tall blonde woman exited one of the stalls eyeing Clair as she sat rubbing the soles of her feet. "Sore feet?"

"Evening, Emmerson. My feet haven't been this sore since…" Clair paused and raised her eyes to the roof, the cogs in her brain ticking over. "Nope, they have never been this sore. Ever."

Emmerson giggled and pulled a scarlet-red lipstick out of her purse and began pulling distorted faces in the mirror as she made touch ups. "Well, like

210

I always say, women should wear them more often. That way they'll be used to them when it comes to occasions like tonight."

"Couldn't agree more," Leah said joining Emmerson at the mirror. "We were just talking the other day about how we should start a business here in town, teaching women about fashion and beauty. Isn't that right, Em?"

"Ah huh." Emmerson nodded. "It's like I've been saying, if there were fashion police, some of the women in this town would end up in jail. I wouldn't be caught dead in some of the outfits they go around town in. Leah and I even started a graduate diploma in fashion and textiles, proving that we've got what it takes to make it."

Clair lowered her head to hide her smile. They meant well and they had hearts of gold, but the fashion police? Clair replaced her shoes and stood. "I guess I'll head back to the celebrations," she said, realising the ladies hadn't even heard her speak above their conversation. It was as if she were invisible. *I'll leave you to your fashion problems. I've more important fish to fry.*

"Take that Christina Jacobs, for instance," Leah said, shock emanating in her words. "That outfit she has on this evening is gorgeous and she has the figure to do it justice, but the colour is positively disgraceful. No-one in their right mind wears tangerine anymore, especially mixed with barf green."

Emmerson cut in. "I know, shocking. My dad was telling me just this morning she had the nerve to try and cheat on her taxes."

Christina lying on her taxes? What is it with people in this town, have good old-fashioned morals gone out the window? Don't they know how to tell the truth anymore?

Emmerson continued, "Apparently, she tried to claim some public relations course she was supposed to be doing over at Watson's Creek, but she didn't even take it."

Clair froze and her ears pricked as Emmerson's words slammed into her chest. The hairs on the back of her neck stood to attention. Her mind was working double time. Was that the same public relations course James Hapworth was supposed to be taking? Come to think of it, Clair remembered Christina leaving James' Watson Creek office last week, when she was in town buying supplies. Clair pinched the bridge of her nose. She seemed to have more questions than answers.

Were they in it together? Maybe Christina was the woman James referred to in the message, but why did he want to change her mind? About what? What if she made up the whole curse nonsense about the Sweets mansion and why did she print that garbage in the paper, depicting me as a killer? Is she covering for the real killer? A darkened thought shattered her very being. Is *she* the killer? *The missing phone.* Thanks to Detective Anderson being so open in the spirit of cooperation, Christina was the only other person who knew about James' missing phone. Why hasn't she printed that in her paper? Why keep it a secret? Unless she has an ulterior motive.

Could the murderer really be Christina Jacobs? Clair's thoughts were starting to form a tangled mess inside her mind. While she didn't have all the answers, there were too many coincidences to let Christina walk away without finding out her side of the story. Adrenaline shot through her veins as she raced out of the ladies'. *I think you and I need to have another talk, Christina Jacobs. And this time I will get the answers I need.*

Clair's heart raced and her cheeks hurt from smiling as she dodged guests, compliments, and heartfelt embraces on her way back to the ballroom. *They've already unveiled the cupcake display?*

Charlotte had come up with a unique cupcake design depicting an original Ashton Point as it had been, back when old Peaberry first discovered it. It seemed by the overwhelming accolades she was receiving, it had been a huge success. A success Clair would revel in *after* she found Christina.

Clair threw her arms up in the air in exasperation. "Where are you, Mason?" she muttered straining to look above the crowded room for his striking physique.

"Clair, what's wrong," Charlotte asked as she joined her sister, her brow creased with concern.

Clair felt the blood drain from her face as she spotted a ball of tangerine and barf green heading for the exit. *Christina?*

"Clair, what's going on?" Charlotte demanded. "You look like you've seen a ghost. Are you all right?"

"Yes, I'm fine," she snapped, brushing Charlotte's concern away. *But my chance to get some real answers is about to walk out the door.* "Have you seen Mason?"

"No, not for some time. I know he was on the dance floor earlier, first with Emmerson and then with Christina."

Clair's gaze whipped to Charlotte's worried expression. "He was dancing with Christina Jacobs?"

Charlotte nodded. "Until I rescued him."

Anger burned deep in her gut. Clair could only imagine what lies that woman had fed Mason. Lies and deception, fuelled by murder. Her pulse raced. She turned to Charlotte and grabbed her shoulders, looking directly into her widened eyes. "Listen very carefully. I have to go and check out a hunch. If you see Mason can you ask him to call me? I'll try and call him on the way."

"What hunch? A hunch about the murderer?"

Clair nodded. "Yes."

Charlotte's eyes widened. "You know who it is don't you?"

"Yes, I think so."

"Who is it?" Charlotte asked eagerly.

Clair shook her head, a sliver of doubt entered her mind. "I'm not a hundred percent sure. I have to go before I miss my chance to find out. Tell Mason to call me."

"Wait, I'll come with you, let me tell Liam," Charlotte said, determination laced her words.

"There's no time. Besides, I could be wrong. We can't both leave, you know they always expect us to come up after the speeches to say something about the cake display. It will look bad if neither of us are here. You stay. After all, it was your amazing creative skills that came up with such a fantastic design attributed to our town's founder. Just please find Mason and tell him to call me and I'll fill him in."

"Okay, go," she said with a shooing action. "I'll take care of Mason, just be careful."

Clair nodded and swallowed around the lump in her throat as she hugged her sister tight before turning to leave.

Chapter Thirteen

PANIC GRIPPED MASON hard. He hadn't seen Clair in over thirty minutes and he was beside himself with worry. She missed the unveiling of her cupcake display. They'd worked so hard on getting it just right, he knew something was wrong when she didn't front.

An icy finger traced Mason's spine as he caught sight of an anxious Charlotte hovering by the entry door, searching the guests. He made a beeline for her, Charlotte's eyes honing in on him as he approached.

"Charlotte, have you seen Clair? I can't find her anywhere."

"Mason, there you are. She's gone," Charlotte said gripping her purse.

Fear clutched his chest. *Gone, what does she mean gone?*

"She left to follow a hunch." Mason struggled to keep up with her. "She was talking about how she may have figured out the murderer, but she couldn't

217

find you and then she rattled off something about how someone was going to trade barf-green for prison-green…"

"Whoa, whoa, whoa. Back up," he said his heart thrashing inside his chest. "Did you say barf green?"

Charlotte nodded.

"Thanks to Emerson and her annoying babble, there's only one person wearing barf-green this evening. She thinks Christina, from *The Chronicle*, is the killer, but why?"

"Christina? No way," Charlotte said in shock. "She didn't actually say, she just said that she had a suspicion."

"Why did she leave?" Mason asked.

"I don't know, but she wanted you to call her."

Mason whipped out his phone and dialled Clair's number, each unanswered ring playing havoc with his nerves. "Come on, Clair…pick up," he muttered under his breath.

No answer. His fingers moved at double pace, dialling her number once more. *This is crazy, why leave?* There was only one reason he could think of that she would leave and that is if Christina did. He searched the room for barf green, but she was nowhere in sight. His whole body tensed. "No answer."

"You don't think she's in real danger, do you?" Charlotte asked, her eyes clouded with worry.

Yes, I do. "I'm not waiting around to find out," he muttered, his fingers punching buttons on his phone. Mason rocked back and forth on his feet waiting impatiently. A gruff voice answered. "Detective, its Mason Hapworth here."

"What can I do for you, Mr Hapworth, I'm extremely busy," Anderson barked.

Mason continued. "I have a problem and I'm hoping you can help me."

"At the moment, my problem is investigating a break-in at your father's place of business in Watson's Creek. It seems whoever worked over your house did the same to his office. I'm in the process of investigating a possible lead. I'm pretty sure it's linked to his murder."

Break-in? Mason's blood ran cold. "Actually, I'm worried about Clair McCorrson. She left the dinner and I'm not exactly sure where she went. I was

hoping you might be able to help me locate her."
There was a long pause on the end of the line and
Mason's stomach dropped.

"Clair McCorrson, you say?"

"Yes, I've tried to ring her but she doesn't seem
to be answering," Mason said impatiently.

"Mmm, I did receive two garbled messages
from her about twenty minutes ago, but I haven't
been able to raise her on the phone to find out what's
going on," he said in a frustrated tone.

Bile rose in Mason's throat as his words sank
in. "What do you mean garbled message? What did
she say?"

"Listen, why don't you meet me at the station
in about forty-five minutes and you can listen to the
messages yourself?" he asked.

Forty-five minutes, it might be too late by then. Sweat
beaded his forehead and a cold chill set deep in his
body. "No," he snapped. "You may be willing to wait,
but I'm not. Please, Detective, I need to know what
she said and you did promise to keep me apprised of
all developments in the case."

An impatient sigh echoed down the line. "That, I did. Clair wasn't very clear in her messages, but the gist of them indicated she had a strong hunch who murdered both your father and Roland Trent, but she didn't say who."

That's old news. "Is that all?" Mason asked, his pulse racing.

"Pretty much. In her second message, she mumbled something about how important it was to go back the where it all started to find the answers. I'll be tied up for a little while longer here, but I have an officer following it up. I'll be in touch if I have any news," Detective Anderson said and rung off.

Mason huffed, the frustration that burned in his belly was now replaced with worry. He pocketed his phone and turned to Charlotte.

"What did he say?" she asked.

"He received two messages from Clair, although they weren't very clear. She said something about how important it was to go back to where it all started to find the answers." His eyes narrowed. "What did she mean by that?"

Charlotte shrugged and shook her head, her fingers nervously fiddling with the clasp on her sapphire and diamond necklace.

"Where it all started," he muttered to himself, rubbing his temple in an effort to alleviate the pounding throb.

Charlotte gasped and her jaw dropped. Her eyes widening with realisation. "Oh, no. She couldn't have?"

His gaze shot to hers. "Couldn't have what?"

Charlotte's eyes darkened. "Think about it, Mason. Where did this whole nightmare begin?" She paused and he shook his head. "It all started when she stumbled across the body…at the Sweets Mansion. She's gone *back* to where it all started."

"The Sweets Mansion… but why?"

Charlotte slapped her forehead. "How could I have been so stupid? She must have followed Christina. So, if Clair is at the Sweets Mansion, then so is Christina. If Clair's hunch is right, she's about to walk into an empty house, in the dead of night, with a murderer."

Mason's heart forgot to beat as he barricaded images of Clair in danger from his mind. *How had the evening gotten so out of hand so quickly?* There wasn't time to waste, he had to find Clair, and fast.

"Hey, you, what's going on?" Liam asked as he sidled up beside Charlotte.

The fear bleeding through Mason's veins bolted him into action. "I'm heading to the Sweets place to find Clair. I'll call Detective Anderson on the way, but I need you to call the police station and have someone meet me there."

"Police?" Liam said, confusion blanked his expression.

Charlotte nodded. "Right. What if they won't believe me?"

"Make them," he said edging toward the exit. "I don't care what you have to do, go down to the police station and drag them there if you have to, just get them there. It could mean the difference between life and death for Clair."

****

Clair took a deep breath, relishing the sting of the cool, salty evening air as it filtered through her car. "What are you up to?" she whispered, her hands gripping the steering wheel tight.

She'd tailed Christina from the Gala dinner to *The Chronicle*, where she'd stopped for less than five minutes. Then she'd gone through the suburban streets and finally to the Sweets Mansion. "So, you've come back to the scene of the crime."

Clair parked her car a few doors down, out of Christina's line of sight. She stared straight ahead, her shoulders stiff and her jaw set. Up until today this place had been a crime scene. "I guess you're looking for that one bit of evidence that will put you behind bars." *The phone.* "If the police couldn't find it here, what makes you think you can?"

Clair eased her hand on the cool metal of the door handle, ready to confront the one woman that held her freedom in the palm of her hands. An invisible claw of danger washed over her and her gut tightened.

Am I seriously going to follow a potential murderer into an empty house? How else was she going to find out the truth? If Christina found the phone first, she could destroy it, blowing any chance of them linking her to the murders. Clair got out and locked her car, easing the strap of her handbag over her head and across her chest so it wouldn't fall off her shoulder. She shivered, the evening had taken a cool turn, the fresh smell of summer rain looming. She looked toward the clear night sky. "Please don't rain, at least not yet."

Having had no luck in reaching Detective Anderson while she waited at *The Chronicle*, she dialled Detective Anderson one more time. "Come on, pick up," she muttered under her breath. Anderson's gruff voice bellowed down the line.

"This is Detective Anderson, I'm unable to take your call, but please leave a message and I'll be in touch soon."

Another message? But will he get it in time? "Detective Anderson this is Clair McCorrson, again. I think I may have worked out who the killer is. I know you won't believe me unless I can prove it. That's where I am now, trying to get the evidence. I'll be in touch when I have proof. I'm back to where it all started." Whatever Christina was up to wouldn't wait, maybe Clair was already too late.

It's now or never.

A shiver ran down her spine as the cool evening breeze brushed against her body. Her legs were like plasticine, ready to crumble at any minute, but she kept placing one foot in front of the other until she was standing at the bottom of the front steps, her heart pounding in her chest.

The eerie silence of the stark night echoed so loud in her ears it was as if every minuscule noise was amplified a billion decibels, including her heart beat. Why wouldn't her feet move? Surely the prospect of freedom was worth the risk?

A sudden crash from inside the house robbed her of her next breath. Gasping, her hand flew to cover her mouth and her eyes widened in alarm. *What was that?* Clair froze to the spot, her gaze locking on to the slim beam of light seeping from an upstairs window. A surge of energy bolted through her veins. If she went in now, there was no chance Christina would see her, since she was upstairs.

Please, please let this nightmare end tonight.

Clair walked up the stairs as if on eggshells, her chest so tight with anxiety she could barely breathe. Her mind conjured up a scene from the old

Hitchcock classic, *Psycho*, as Detective Arbogast entered Norman's house before ascending to the top of the stairs where his life is abruptly ended.

Clair held her breath, her eyes widening at the semi-open door, just enough to squeeze through. She held her body rigid and edged her way in as if the door and frame were hot lava that would disintegrate her body with the slightest touch.

She'd forgotten she was holding her breath until her lungs burned for air. It took a moment for her eyes to adjust to the darkness of the foyer. The only source of light was the stream of moonlight through the window, which was lighting the bottom of the staircase. She could see the deadened image of James Hapworth as clear in her mind as the day she stumbled across his body. The floor still housed a faint stain of blood. Her hand clutched her stomach. *I think I'm going to be sick.*

Footsteps above her head shook her back to the present and this little adventure would be for nothing if Christina found her before she could get the evidence she needed. Triumph filled her as she spotted a mass of boxes piled up to the right of the staircase. She hadn't noticed them on her last visit. A perfect hiding place. Careful to conceal herself from view of the stairs she bolted toward the boxes. The smell of the dust and musty wood filled her nostrils and scratched at her throat.

Her pulse intensified and the seconds ticked over as she waited, Christina's footsteps continued to pound the floorboards above. *Why would James' phone be upstairs?* If she murdered James, it's not like she'd fess up voluntarily.

A moment passed and a thought struck her. *I've got it, I'll record her on my Smartphone. Why didn't I think of it earlier?* She felt like kicking herself in the backside. Her absentmindedness could have cost her dearly. Clair eased her hand into her handbag, in the dark her fingers searched for her phone.

Her heart lurched when she saw five missed calls from Mason. She shook the chill in her body off, checked her phone was still on silent from the dinner and set it to record.

"Right, now, it's only a matter of time before you stuff up and I'll be here to record everything," she whispered, chuffed with herself. She really should call Mason, but her gaze shot to a muffled noise coming from the top of the stairs while her heart skipped a beat. *Sorry, Mason, you'll just have to wait, it's show time.*

"Come on, James, I know you did this deliberately. Where is it?" Christina muttered to herself as she descended the staircase.

Clair froze, straining to hear Christina's words. *Did what deliberately?* Her gaze checked her phone was recording once more before returning it to her bag. Clair peeked out from behind the stack of boxes, careful to keep out of the beam of Christina's torch and watched eagerly. She committed Christina's every movement to memory. In her desperation to find the missing item, she carelessly threw antiquated trinkets left, right and centre. Drop cloths covering the pieces of remaining furniture suddenly hit the floor as Christina grew more desperate.

"What have you done with it, James? It wasn't at your house or your office. It's not like you could have taken your phone to the grave with you." Christina pulled the dresser drawers out, recklessly sifting through the contents piece by piece.

Clair squinted straining to see through the limited moonlight. *I was right, she is after his phone.* The pieces of the puzzle seemed to fall into place at lightning speed. *Oh, my goodness, it* was *you.* It was Christina who'd ransacked Stella's house searching for the phone and what better time to come and search the scene of the crime when the whole town is at the Founder's Day gala dinner?

Clair felt the room start to spin around her. She barely noticed the pitter-patter of rain that dotted the roof. Christina had done her best to discredit her, place the blame on her, all to cover up her own evil actions. Clair eased her elbow on the smaller box in front of her, hoping to keep Christina in view as she continued her search of the floor beside the staircase. Within seconds her elbow drove straight through the empty box. She hit the floor with a thud, landing on her hip bone, pain shooting up her spine. She gasped, nausea rolling around in her gut.

Christina spun, her eyes squinting shooting pitchforks in Clair's direction. "Who's there? Come on, show yourself," she demanded shining her torch straight into Clair's eyes.

"Okay, all right," Clair said as she threw her hand up to stop the blinding beam. "Do you think you could take that torch out of my eyes?"

"Clair McCorrson?" Christina said in a stunned tone. "What are you doing here?"

Her sudden predicament had her chest in knots. She was defenceless and within meters of a murderer. If she stayed on the floor, she'd be a sitting duck. Clair ignored the pain in her lower back and slowly began to push her body off the floor.

"Stop right there," Christina barked.

Clair froze for a moment but refused to be the victim in this scenario. "Come on, Christina, I'm only standing up so we can chat like civilised people," she said easing herself to a standing position.

Goose bumps assaulted her body as Christina's gaze drilled into her. "What are you doing here?"

"I could ask you the same question," Clair said folding her arms across her chest, praying her phone was still recording. "I watched you at the dinner. You were as nervous as a baby foal taking its first steps and it was obvious you were hiding something. So, I followed you when you left the dinner so abruptly, but never in a million years would I have guessed you could kill anyone in cold blood."

"Don't be ridiculous. I don't know what you're talking about." Christina nervously rocked from one foot to the other.

Clair's mind whirled a mile a minute despite the churning in her stomach caused by Christina's skittish behaviour. Her eyes widened and fear shot up her spine as Christina edged herself toward the small side table, her eyes shooting between Clair and the door. "I think it's about time the truth came out, and besides it's just you and me. Who else is here to listen?" Clair could almost hear her heart beating in the silence as Christina mulled over her offer. "I know you killed James and Roland Trent, but what I don't know is why."

A smirk gleamed across Christina's face and she laughed, an evil sound that echoed around the foyer. The next words out of her mouth chilled Clair to the core. "Why not? You're no match for me. I've already taken care of one back-stabbing nuisance." She shrugged. "What's one more?"

Clair couldn't believe her luck. The words spilled from her lips. "So, you admit you killed James?"

Christina huffed. "Good old James, ha. Yes, I killed him and I'd do it again in a heartbeat."

Holy cow, she actually admitted it. That was way too easy.

"That lying piece of garbage." Christina narrowed her eyes at Clair. "You know, for months he had the gall to string me along, telling me that he was going to leave that woman, telling me how much he loved me and how I was the only woman he really cared about and he was going to marry me. Then I find out he had no intention of leaving her. I was the other woman and he was dumping me? Suddenly, I'm not good enough, I'm yesterday's trash. Well no-one throws me away and gets away with it."

Clair's brow creased. "You killed him because he dumped you? It had nothing to do with your taxes?"

"My taxes?" Christina said in a high-pitched tone. "Don't be stupid, my taxes are the least of my worries. I killed him because he was going to run off with the money *we* worked so hard to swindle, and share it with that woman and no good piece of garbage, Roland Trent. He was going to leave me with nothing. That's why Roland had to go as well. I couldn't leave the one person alive who could destroy everything with his big mouth."

I don't believe this? She framed me for murder over money and a lover's spat. Clair's feet were frozen to the spot. Her fists clenched so hard in anger that her nails dug into her palms. The increased drone of the rain on the roof was grating on her nerves. "I don't understand. Why would you frame me? What did I ever do to you? And what about that nonsense about the curse on this house? There is no curse, is there?" Clair asked through gritted teeth.

"Master stroke of genius, if I do say so myself. If I had all the time in the world, I couldn't have planned it better." Christina let out a stifled giggle that riled Clair. "You walked straight into it. You were the classic fall guy, all I had to do was plant a few doubts about you in the community, make up that curse baloney, run a few articles that painted you as a killer and sit back and wait for you to be arrested.

Murdering Roland and leaving his body behind your shop, his shirt smeared with cupcake icing from the cupcakes you left here was just an added bonus. What I didn't plan on was James' phone disappearing."

"What's the phone got to do with anything?" Clair asked, determined to find out the whole truth.

"Everything," she snapped picking up a lone candlestick from the small wooden table. Her eyes focused on the brass object in her hands. "You know what's so ironic?"

Round object, the base the size of a wine bottle. Clair shook her head, a cold chill engulfing her limbs. "What?"

"It's almost like a game of Cluedo, with history repeating itself." She laughed and raised the pitch of her voice like a Hollywood movie trailer. "James Hapworth, in the foyer with the candlestick. Roland Trent, in the alley with the same candlestick. It seems you're going to meet the same untimely death. After all, I can't have you telling the truth, now can I? It would spoil my perfect ending."

Clair's heart jumped into her throat as Christina raised the candlestick above her head and took a step toward her. Throwing up her hands, she yelled, "Wait. If you're going to kill me anyway, the least you can do is tell me the whole truth. What's so important about the phone?"

"Oh, for goodness sake," she said dropping her arms down. "Fine, what's a few more seconds?"

Seconds…seconds? What can I do in seconds? Now she was regretting not waiting for Mason. Her blood was pumping so fast she thought her brain would explode. If only she had her can of mace in her bag, she could disarm Christina long enough to escape. Clair carefully angled the right side of her body away from Christina's view. She paused, waiting for her to be so wrapped up in the sound of her own voice that she wouldn't notice Clair's slight movement. Easing her hand into her bag, Clair's heart exploded in her chest when her hand encircled a small deodorant-like cylinder at the bottom of her handbag. It wasn't mace but it was the next best thing. She'd only get one chance to make it count.

"I used the other candlestick to kill James and it's now sitting at the bottom of John's Cape. I threw it in the water after Roland met his end. As for James' phone, it's my ticket to retirement. I find the phone, I'm set for life. You see, my dear, Clair, not only does it have some pictures of James and I in compromising positions, it has private emails about some of our rather dubious business transactions that even his partner wasn't privy to. But the most important piece of information is the passwords and account details for the money he embezzled from his company. Five million dollars and with you out of the way, it will all be mine." Christina raised the candlestick above her head and charged in Clair's direction.

Clair's heart pounded against her ribcage. Christina's face turned hard and the sinister glare in her eyes was only surpassed by her evil words. "Prepare to join James in hell."

Jerking back, Clair held her breath, butting up against the stack of boxes, trapped, seconds from the end of her life. Clair's blood froze, her gaze fixed to the silver candlestick poised above Christina's head ready to strike.

Now! Clair flung her hand out of her bag, cylinder clutched in her hand thrusting it toward the advancing woman.

Her heart leapt into her throat as she squeezed the trigger. Whoosh. A steady stream of metallic gold glitter dust shot into Christina's eyes. She stopped, throwing her hand up to protect her eyes, the candlestick tumbling to the ground with a clang.

"Ahhhhhh," Christina screamed unable to keep her eyes open much longer. Stumbling off balance, Christina toppled into the boxes. Clair jumped out of the falling line just in time.

"Ah, my eyes. My eyes," Christina wailed, her arms flailing around like a fish out of water. Clair took off for the front door, not bothering to look back, her body on auto pilot. The faint echo of sirens in the distance struggled to breach the now pelting barrage of rain on the roof. Clair took a deep breath. The suffocating air outside clogged her chest. The rain had made the warm summer evening turn muggy and humid. It was like being wrapped in a wool blanket on a hot summer day.

Clair's gaze turned as the screech of Christina's voice rung out from inside. "There's no use running."

Like I want to run all the way to the police station with Christina hot on my heels. She scanned for the perfect hiding place and spotted a planter box housing a tall overgrown bamboo plant at the end of the porch. *Perfect.* Clair waited for what felt like forever until finally she breathed a sigh of relief at the crescendo of sirens and flashing lights that came to rest on the verge, it was like opening night of the Royal Show. Triumph filled her chest as Robert and Mason both sprinted from separate cars toward the porch. But before she could stand, Christina took the stage one more time.

"Oh, thank goodness you're here. You have to help me," Christina sobbed, her hands moving like the wind fanning her face. "I thought I was going to die for sure. Clair McCorrson tried to kill me."

Clair saw red. *I did what? How dare she turn the tables and blame me?*

"What are you talking about?" Mason demanded, his eyes wide.

"Calm down," Robert said eyeing Mason to behave and leave the questioning to a professional. "Now, take it slow and tell me what happened."

"I-I-I was on my way home from the dinner as I wasn't feeling well and I spotted Clair McCorrson looking suspicious. So, I followed her and she came here and I knew she was up to no good. After all why would she come here, to this place, after what happened, unless she was hiding something? I cornered her and she confessed to killing James and Roland. She was going to frame me for their murders." Christina began to hyperventilate, giving the impression of the perfect victim.

This is crazy, hasn't this woman made my life hell enough?

Mason stepped back and folded his arms across his chest. "That's ridiculous. Clair is the most amazing, wonderful woman I've ever met. She doesn't have an evil bone in her body and to accuse her of trying to kill you is just plain ludicrous. Where's your evidence?" he asked.

Clair paused a moment and let her gaze wonder over Mason as he fiercely defended her. She couldn't get over just how handsome he looked in his white dinner shirt and tie. His trust in her was infallible and she'd be stupid to let him leave town without telling him how she felt. She smiled at the flutter of butterflies in her stomach.

"I'm telling you the truth." Christina continued her babbling as she thrust out her arm. "See, look at these scratches. She attacked me and when I tried to defend myself, she threw me into a pile of boxes to escape. She's probably not far. If you go now you'll probably catch her."

Trepidation pitted in the base of her belly as Robert looked like he was starting to believe her lies. She couldn't, no she wouldn't let Christina call the shots any more.

"I'll give *you* the truth," she whispered. Clair pulled her phone out of her bag and her chest warmed when she saw that it was still recording. She stopped it and reset it mid-way through and prayed when she hit play it would be Christina's confession.

Clair slowly stood from behind the planter box and held her breath as she hiked up the volume and hit the play button.

"Why not? You're no match for me. I've already taken care of one back-stabbing nuisance. What's one more?"

"So, you admit you killed James?"

"Good old James, ha. Yes, I killed him and I'd do it again in a heartbeat."

241

Three sets of eyes flew to the sound of the recording as she slowly edged herself toward them. Mason's blue eyes met hers and she felt a shiver zing up her spine.

"What is that?" Christina asked her face pale.

"That lying piece of garbage. You know, for months he had the gall to string me along, telling me that he was going to leave that woman, telling me how much he loved me and how I was the only woman he really cared about and he was going to marry me. Then I find out he had no intention of leaving her. I was the other woman and he was dumping me? Suddenly, I'm not good enough, I'm yesterday's trash. Well no-one throws me away and gets away with it."

"Sounds like a confession to me," Robert said as he pulled his handcuffs from his belt.

Christina's face turned beetroot red. "Why, you little cow. Of all the deceitful, underhanded things to do. How dare you record me without my permission? I know my rights."

Robert held his hand up to silence Mason. "So, you're denying the allegations of murder?"

"Of course, I am," Christina snapped folding her arms.

"Even though they're as plain as day and at least three people have heard you confess to the murder?"

Christina paled as her guilty words continued.

"I used the other candlestick and it is now at the bottom of John's Cape. I threw it in the water after Roland met his end. As for James' phone, it's my ticket to retirement. I find the phone, I'm set for life. You see, my dear Clair, not only does it have some pictures of James and I in compromising positions, it has private emails about some of our rather dubious business transactions that even his business partner wasn't privy to. But the most important piece of information is the passwords and account details for the money he embezzled from his company. Five million dollars and with you out of the way, it will all be mine."

A smile spread across Robert's face and he winked at Clair. He tapped his handcuffs in his palm. "You see, Ms Jacobs, this is what we call a reliable source. And it appears there is incriminating evidence on the victims' phone, regarding dubious emails and allegations of embezzlement. Most importantly, it points to you as the murderer and something about a candlestick at the bottom of John's Cape, which could be the murder weapon. I have no doubt it can be retrieved by police divers."

Christina's jaw dropped and her face reddened.

Robert continued, his tone a little cheerier than it should be when arresting another human being. "And now, if you'll accompany me down to the station, I think Detective Anderson will probably have a few questions."

Clair couldn't be sure if it was from embarrassment at being caught or the humidity of the evening rainstorm, but perspiration beaded Christina's forehead. Either way, triumph bled through Clair's veins. Finally, the nightmare was over.

"Never," Christina blurted as she sidestepped Robert and ran down the porch stairs into the pelting rain in her cream suede stilettos, toward the street. Her escape abruptly stopped as another police car pulled up.

Robert sighed and threw his hands up in the air. "Seriously, why do they always run?" he asked, shrugging his shoulders.

Before he could give chase, Detective Anderson cut her off as he stepped out of his car.

Christina darted to the right and tried to escape out the driveway instead of the garden gate, but Anderson was too quick and blocked her exit.

A giggle erupted from deep within Clair's chest and she was quickly joined by Mason. His hearty laugh warmed her heart.

"Hey, Loughlin, get your backside down here and help me," Anderson called as he gave chase.

Robert shrugged again. "Duty calls."

It was like watching an episode of *Two Broke Girls* with Han Lee and Oleg chasing Caroline Channing around the diner, hoping to score a kiss.

"I don't think I've laughed this hard in a long time," Mason said as he rubbed the side of his belly.

"Me neither. Feels good to laugh after such a horrible week."

Mason threaded his fingers through hers and pulled her toward the swing chair at the other end of the porch. "Come, sit with me. Let's enjoy the show."

Clair couldn't deny the way her stomach flip-flopped when his hand held hers. She could feel the heat from his hand work its way up her arm and she was suddenly more intensely aware of him than ever before.

"Sure," she said, trying her best to cover her butterflies. Her attention was torn between Mason's charismatic pull and the entertainment playing out before her on the front lawn.

The game of cat and mouse quickly came to an abrupt halt when Christina's heel snagged on the soaking grass and she catapulted head-first into the muddy garden bed. Clair's stomach shook as she laughed and a sharp pain shot across her belly. "Oh, this is just too good. Wait 'til I tell Charlotte. She'll be on the ground rolling in hysterics."

Although the rain seemed to be easing, all three were drenched, as if they'd just walked through a waterfall. Robert handcuffed her and pulled Christina up while he spoke to Detective Anderson. He eventually led Christina to his patrol car, her mouth motoring along one-hundred miles an hour. A sight Clair would never forget. *That will teach you to mess with a McCorrson.*

Mason stood, his shoulders squared as Detective Anderson joined them on the porch.

"There appears to be a new development in my father's murder. Wouldn't you agree, Detective?"

Anderson and Mason stared each other down. "So, it seems."

Clair wiped her clammy palms down her thighs. She half-smiled. "Perfect timing, Detective Anderson. Did Robert explain the situation?"

"Yes, indeed, he did and while I was off investigating the break-in at Mr Hapworth's place of business, all the action was happening here. Ms Jacobs has some explaining to do." He took his jacket off, dispelling the raindrops with a few calculated shakes. "Robert tells me he has a reliable source that can provide evidence indicating Christina was here at this location and he believed there was enough evidence incriminating her in the murders. Is that the way it happened?"

Clair swallowed the lump in her throat and nodded. "Who am I to challenge the word of one of Ashton Point's finest officers?"

"I see. You know you put yourself in a very precarious position this evening," he said, sliding his arms back into his jacket. "You were very lucky."

Mason shook his head and said, "I wouldn't call it luck, but I am very thankful that she came out unscathed." His gaze caught hers and he brushed a stray strand of hair off her face.

She smiled up at him and they both stood in silence.

Detective Anderson cleared his throat. "Listen, this is the second murder one of you McCorrson ladies has inadvertently solved. Can we make it the last? Otherwise, I'll have to file for early retirement if you're going to do my job for me."

Clair chuckled. "Suits me just fine."

Mason piped up. "I'd like to keep her in one piece for a while longer."

Anderson continued. "I'm sure you know the drill by now. I'll require you to come down to the station to make a statement about the events of this evening."

Mason frowned. "Tonight?"

Clair encircled Mason's hand with hers and rubbed her thumb over the back of his palm. She smiled at his startled expression. "I don't mind," she said softly. "It's not like I'm in any mood to head back to the dinner, but I wouldn't mind a lift. If it's no trouble."

She barely heard Detective Anderson's goodbye, her focus was solely on the man that could possibly be the answer to her dreams. If she could persuade him to stick around town. A variety of words tried to battle their way from her brain to her mouth, but she struggled to string any together in a sentence.

Mason looked thoughtful for a few seconds and Clair could feel the heat where her hand held his. "I'm not usually this forthcoming, but would you mind terribly if I kissed you again?" he asked with a glint in his eye.

No, absolutely not. Definitely not. You'll get no argument from me. "I could think of nothing I'd like more than for you to kiss me."

Mason's hand entwined in her hair and he pulled her toward him. Their lips met eagerly and her arms snaked around his neck, her body pressed in close to his. His lips were warm and they tasted of sweet caramel. *Mmm, yum.* Her body hummed to life under his touch, he'd reawakened something inside her that had lain dormant for years.

Reluctantly, she pulled away and gazed up at him and her heart did a somersault inside her chest at just how handsome he was, especially when he wore his sexy glasses. Clair fought the urge to pull him close and kiss him again.

Oh Goodness, please don't let me make a fool of myself, let him like me as much as I like him. Clair took a deep breath and bit the bottom of her lip. "What will you do now? Head back to Surfers?" she asked.

"Oh, I don't know. I was thinking of sticking around for a while." A sly smile worked its way across his face. "You see, I have a crush on a stunning red-head here in town. She's beautiful, intelligent and her sister's cupcakes are to die for and I was thinking of asking her out. I'm just not sure if she'd say yes or break my heart."

On the inside, Clair wanted to jump up and down and do backflips, but on the outside, she smiled and calmly said, "Someone once said, *if there is no risk, there will be no reward.* I think I can safely say if you take the chance, your reward and your heart with be very grateful."

Mason gave a chuckle. "I guess I'll also need to speak to step-mother dearest. There's still a lot to sort out."

Clair's hand muffled a gasp and her eyes widened.

Concern marred Mason's expression. "What is it? What's wrong?"

"I'm such a dingbat, in the excitement of the day I only got a chance to tell you about the break-in. I completely forgot to tell you the most important part." She could kick herself for her absentmindedness.

"Tell me what?"

"It was all a lie. Stella made the whole marriage up. She fessed up that she forged the marriage certificate to stop you getting your hands on his money. She admitted to knowing Roland Trent and bribed him with half the money to keep quiet."

He huffed. "His dirty money, you mean. I want no part of it."

"Not the life insurance policy. The three million is all yours." He paused and Clair's heart warmed at the way Mason's face lit up when her words finally sank in. "Stella admitted to forging her name on the policy. You are the rightful beneficiary and it proves that your father did love you, in his own way."

"I guess he did," he said.

She nodded. "You know what this means, don't you?" Before she could answer, Mason wrapped his arms around her, yanked her up and spun her in circles on the porch, her feet dangling mid-air.

"Mason, for goodness' sake, what has gotten into you?"

"You," he said loosening his grip and lowering her to the ground. He tilted her head back and looked straight into her eyes. "You've gotten into me, Clair McCorrson, and with my worry about money taken care of, I'm free to live wherever I want, and I choose Ashton Point."

"You mean it?" she asked, her eyes widening.

"Cross my heart," he said making a fake cross on his chest. "With all the excitement that happens around here, it's a good thing I'll be sticking around. Although, I'll be happy if we can stay away from dead bodies from now on."

"Promise." Clair snuggled closer, satisfaction spreading in her veins. Life was definitely looking up. In the last few months Ashton Point had seen enough drama for two lifetimes, what else could possibly go wrong?

The End

Thank you for reading **Cupcakes and Curses**
If you enjoyed this story, I would really appreciate it
if you would consider leaving a review of this book,
no matter how short, at the retailer site where you
bought your copy or on sites like Goodreads.

YOU are the key to this book's success and the
success of **The Cupcake Capers Cozy Mystery
Series.** I read every review and they really do make
a huge difference.

Keep up to date on Polly's book releases, signings
and events on her website:
https://www.pollyholmesmysteries.com

About the Author

Polly Holmes is the cheeky, sassy alter ego of P.L. Harris. When she's not writing her next romantic suspense novel as P.L. Harris, she is planning the next murder in one of Polly's cozy mysteries.

According to Polly, the best part about writing a cozy mystery is researching. Finding the best way to hook the reader, a great way to murder someone, a plethora of suspects and of course a good dose of sweet treats thrown in for good measure.

Polly lives not far from the beach in the northern suburbs of Perth, Western Australia with her Bishion Frise, Bella. When she's not writing you can find her sipping coffee in her favourite cafe, watching reruns of Murder, She Wrote or Psych, or taking long walks along the beach soaking up the fresh salty air.

You can visit *Polly Holmes* at her website: www.pollyholmesmysteries.com

Book 3 Now

Available

Cassidy's Story

Cupcakes and Corpses

When it comes to design, death is in the details.

Cassidy McCorrson has worked hard to develop her reputation as a leading interior designer in her seaside town of Ashton Point. Since arriving home from visiting her parents in New York, her skills have been in high demand. Between juggling the design for her sister's new cupcake shop and her private client, Cassidy barely has time to prepare for the upcoming Christmas celebrations.

Cassidy is excited at the prospect of delivering designs she can be proud of, but her world is turned upside down when the body of a local reporter is found murdered on location at her latest work site. What should have been a straightforward job turns out to be the worst decision of her life.

In order to clear her name and restore her reputation, Cassidy must find the real killer before she ends up redesigning the interior of a jail cell. Can she unearth the killer before time runs out?

Book 1 Now

Available

Charlotte's Story

Cupcakes and Cyanide

Welcome to Ashton Point. One sweet taste could be her last.

Charlotte McCorrson has spent her entire life building her business, CC's Simply Cupcakes. The town of Ashton Point is her home and she's garnered a reputation of stellar service and delightful pastries, one nibble at a time. But everything isn't as sweet in the sleepy, coastal town as Charlotte would like to think. She is in for a rude awakening and no amount of sugar will make this medicine go down any smoother.

After catering a large town-wide event, Ashton Point's morning newspaper fills Charlotte McCorrson with an icy sense of dread. The headlines scream *Cupcake Killer!* and put the blame squarely on CC's Simply Cupcakes. When bodies begin to pile up behind her confectionary goodies, Charlotte must prove that while her cupcakes are delicious, they aren't literally to die for—before she ends up in jail for a crime she didn't commit.

This is Book 1 in The Cupcake Capers Series and may contain elements of humour, drama and danger. However, it will definitely not contain any of the following potentially lethal substances:

Swearing or profanity.

Gore or graphic scenes.

Cliff-hangers or unsolved endings.

Read on for an excerpt of Cupcakes and Cyanide

Chapter One

"CALLING ALL THE single ladies."

Charlotte McCorrson stood nestled at the back of the reception centre, semi-hidden behind a burgundy-and-white, balloon topiary tree.

Great. Bouquet throwing time, just what I need. For every man in the room to know I'm still single. When Beth invited her to the wedding she was over the moon, after all, they'd been good friends since Clair and her family moved to Ashton Point three years ago. What she hadn't planned on was still being single by the time the wedding rolled around.

They may as well take out a front-page ad in the Ashton Point Chronicle. She could see it now. "Ashton Point master cupcake baker extraordinaire struggles to snag herself a husband. Could she be lacking that special ingredient all men are looking for? What is wrong with the redheaded beauty?" She'd been over the moon when Beth and Lincoln asked CC's Simply Cupcakes to design a wedding cake, based around Charlotte's award-winning cupcake designs.

"Charlotte? What are you doing back here?" A petite voice spoke from behind.

She spun, her breath catching as her gaze landed on a vision in white. Decked out in a satin Karen Willis Holmes, floor-length, empire dress with embroidered tulle overlay, Beth looked like an angel. There had barely been a dry eye in the church as she walked down the aisle to her handsome prince. The fairy-tale wedding every bride dreams of.

Charlotte stiffened as Beth threw her arms around her neck and squeezed. "I never got a chance to properly thank you for the wonderful cupcake display you made. It was truly the cake of my dreams. I'm so glad you were able to share my special day with me. It wouldn't have been the same without you and Clair here," she said with a beaming smile.

"You're welcome, I wouldn't have missed it for the world. I'm so happy you liked it," she said in a muffled voice. Her mouth was half covered by blonde ruffles of hair, leaving the metallic taste of hairspray on her tongue.

Beth pulled back and their gazes held strong. "Liked it? Are you serious? I loved it." A bolt of electric energy ran up Charlotte's spine. She cherished the buzz she got from seeing the joy her cupcakes brought others. "And if anyone thinks they're taking the leftovers home tonight, they have another thing coming. That's all I'll be eating 'til we leave for our honeymoon next week."

Both ladies burst into laughter. Beth's happiness was starting to rub off on Charlotte.

"Didn't you hear the MC? You need to get to the dance floor. I'm about to throw the bouquet."

Charlotte cringed at the thought. "No, no, it's fine. I'm really okay sitting back and letting someone else take the limelight." She had planned on falling madly in love with the man of her dreams by the wedding. *I guess life doesn't always go to plan.*

A sliver of disappointment marred Beth's expression. "I can't believe what I'm hearing. Your grandma would be turning in her grave if she knew you were skipping the bouquet toss. You know how she loved tradition."

Warmth filled Charlotte's heart. Her grandmother treasured her independence. She was the reason they'd moved to Ashton Point in the first place.

She shook her head. "I'm happy watching from the sidelines, besides, a mosh pit of single women jumping around like clucking chickens, all vying for their piece of the elusive dream isn't really my idea of fun."

"Now, that's something I'd like to see." A gruff voice echoed in her ear.

"Excuse me?" Charlotte said, spinning to see Lincoln's best man grinning like the Cheshire Cat.

"A mosh pit of single women jumping around like clucking chickens," he said with a cheeky grin. "Definitely something I'd pay money to see."

Beth sighed, rolled her eyes and play-punched him in the shoulder. "Give it a rest, Liam."

Liam… Mmmm. Why is it that all men named Liam are gorgeous? Liam Hemsworth, Liam Neeson. Tanned, tall and handsome, he flashed a half smile at Charlotte and she felt a spike of interest spark in her belly.

Her gaze caught her sister, Clair, waving frantically behind Liam. *Saved by the bell.* "I'm sorry, Beth, but it looks like Clair needs me."

"Charlotte, there you are. I've been looking for you everywhere," Clair said as she joined them, flicking her deep-red ponytail over her shoulder.

"Why, is something wrong?" Alarm hit Charlotte square in the chest. "Please don't tell me we've run out of cupcakes? There should be plenty to go around. I made loads of extras."

Beth folded her arms across her chest and frowned. "Yes, don't tell me we ran out, otherwise the Bridezilla I've kept hidden inside might have to make a guest appearance."

"Bridezilla?" Liam said with a raised eyebrow. "I find that very hard to believe."

"When it comes to Charlotte's cupcakes, you better believe it," she snapped, holding his stern gaze in hers.

"Everyone calm down, there are plenty of cupcakes." Clair smiled and looped her arm through her sisters. "I was looking for Charlotte for the bouquet toss. Nothing better than a little competition between sisters."

A grin spread across Beth's face and she clapped her hands together. "Wonderful. I best go and get ready. Good luck." Beth said as she hurried off.

"This should be a sight to see. I'll let you two ladies get ready. I'd hate to be the one to keep you from your spot in the chicken brood," Liam said with a smile as he strode back to the bridal table at the top of the dance floor.

Clair raised an eyebrow. "Chicken brood?"

"Never mind," Charlotte said, shaking her head.

"Wasn't that the best man?" Clair asked, forcefully guiding Charlotte toward the crowded dance floor.

Charlotte nodded. *Certainly was THE best man.* She let her eyes wander over his retreating figure. Her gaze seemed to have a mind of its own. It made its way down his broad shoulders, to his trim waist and tight derriere. She felt her cheeks grow hot as she imagined what he would look like out of his suit.

"What was his name again?" Clair's words were met with silence. "Earth to Charlotte," she said, flicking Charlotte's forehead as if she were flicking a fly from the back of her hand. "What is his name?" she snapped.

"Oww." Charlotte rubbed her forehead. "All right. I heard you the first time. Liam. His name is Liam."

Charlotte's stomach tightened as Clair elbowed their way to the centre of the dance floor dragging her along for the ride.

"Okay, ladies. Are we ready for the bouquet toss?" The deep, throaty voice of the MC blared out across the room.

Charlotte's body tensed as ear-splitting screams of single women pierced the air. *Oh my, could this be any more embarrassing?*

To top it off, Beyoncé's *Single Ladies* boomed out as Beth took centre stage.

Her breath caught in her throat as her gaze snared Liam's sly grin from the front of the room. *What's with the grin?* Cheers erupted around her and her eyes widened as Beth's bouquet flew straight into her arms.

Charlotte stood in the kitchen, her lungs void of air as the newspaper headline screamed at her like an unwanted nightmare. She held the morning newspaper in her icy fingers. *Cupcake Killer!*

Beth's wedding had been the event of the year, a perfect place to show off her culinary skills. The whole town had turned up to see her finally tie the knot with Lincoln Wade, Ashton Point's most eligible bachelor. Everyone who's anyone had been there, which meant more advertising for their business, CC's Simply Cupcakes.

"I don't believe this." Her hands shook as she read the front-page article. Definitely not the front page she had imagined last night at the wedding. "Why would they think *my* cupcakes killed someone?"

Her eyes were glued to the quote at the bottom of the page next to her picture. *Doctor says two beloved local councilmen are in critical condition and show signs of cyanide poisoning.*

"Cyanide poisoning?" she asked, collapsing on the kitchen stool as her knees gave way. "I do *not* cook with cyanide."

She continued to read. *Guests say that they began feeling ill after the cake was cut and cupcakes distributed.*

"Definitely not from my cupcakes." Anger simmered in her veins. It was going to hit the fan, so to speak, when her sister, Clair, heard of this debacle. Thankfully Cassidy was over visiting Mum and Dad in New York for the next two weeks. At least she won't be tarnished by this nightmare.

This town was their home. They'd moved to Ashton Point on the central coast of New South Wales, just over three years ago to help her grandma. "As if anyone would think I would intentionally poison someone. This is totally unfair," she said, slamming the paper down on the breakfast bar. Her stomach bottoming out as her gaze spotted the bouquet on the kitchen bench.

Clair's weary voice made Charlotte's breath catch in her throat. "What's unfair?" she asked, as she entered the kitchen.

Charlotte's chest tightened like it was being forcibly crushed in a vice. *Damn it, there's no hiding this now.* She scooped up the newspaper before Clair spotted the disaster that was about to tear their dreams apart.

"What's unfair?" Clair repeated heading toward the Nespresso machine and wiping the crusty sleep remnants from the inner rim of her eyes.

Charlotte's pulse sped up. Clearing her throat, she stood and held the newspaper close to her chest, ready to face the music head-on. "I've something to show you, but maybe you should get a coffee and sit down first." Clair was like a five-foot-five, grumpy bed monster with a toothache before her morning coffee.

"For goodness sake, Charlotte, spit it out," she said running her hand through her knotted hair. "I didn't exactly get much sleep last night, by the time we packed up after the wedding."

Charlotte cringed at the mention of the wedding. "You're going to hear about it one way or another." She sighed. "May as well be before you leave the house."

Suspicion worked its way across Clair's face. Leaning against the counter, she folded her arms across her chest. "Okay, enough with the cryptic clues and just tell me what you're talking about."

Charlotte's heart plummeted to the base of her gut. She flipped the paper around and held her breath. Waiting for the incoming explosion.

"Cupcake killer!" Clair's amused, bubbly giggle shot through Charlotte like a dagger. "That's ridiculous. We've known Daniel for three years and everyone in town knows he's big on sensationalising stories without getting his facts straight first. You're not taking that seriously, are you?"

"Of course I'm taking it seriously."

"It's just Daniel trying to big note his career. You and I know there's no truth to it and I'm sure when the truth is revealed, Daniel will be eating his own words." Clair busied herself working her mass of deep-red, bushy hair into a messy bun on the top of her head. "I'm sure it will blow over once they've worked out how they were really poisoned."

Shock bolted through Charlotte's body. "I can't believe you're being so blasé about this. We've worked our butts off to make CC's Simply Cupcakes the best it can possibly be and…" She paused, fury running through her veins. She shook the newspaper in front of Clair's unimpressed expression. "…bad publicity is the last thing we need." Charlotte's stomach grumbled as the fresh scent of roasted hazelnut assaulted her nostrils.

Clair made two fresh cups and handed one off to Charlotte. "Okay, I suppose this isn't ideal, but I'd hardly think one article in the local rag is going to destroy our business. Besides, the whole town knows Daniel will bend the truth to sell one more newspaper."

Clair skimmed over the article. A myriad of emotions flashing across Clair's face made it impossible for Charlotte to determine her thoughts. "They say that no accusations will be acted upon until they have concrete evidence and they'll be following up all leads. Maybe we should keep our eyes and ears open, just in case."

Anxiety crept into Charlotte's mind and compounded her sudden headache into a dull roar. "I agree, but…"

Clair continued, oblivious to Charlotte's annoyance. "And we have Mrs Stevenson's eightieth birthday high tea tomorrow afternoon, down by the river. I'm sure after that goes off without a hitch, Daniel will not only be eating his words, but also your delicious cupcakes."

"Maybe you're right, but I don't think we should wait for the fall out from this article. I know Beth was taking the leftovers home and I don't want her to worry, so I'm going to head over to reassure them that my cupcakes were not the source of the poisoning."

Clair fake coughed. "The morning after their wedding?"

Frustration bubbled up, sending Charlotte's pulse racing. Again. "They're not leaving for their honeymoon 'til Wednesday, and if I remember rightly, Lincoln has to work today to tie up loose ends before they leave."

She glanced one last time at the newspaper and huffed. *This is the most ludicrous thing ever put in print. I'll make you eat your words if it's the last thing I do.*

Clair sighed. "Okay, but don't take too long. I'll be heading over to the shop soon to update the books and make sure we have enough supplies for Mrs Stevenson's order. I'll see you when you get there."

"Okay." Inside, she was furious at Clair's nonchalant attitude. "Mark my words, I'll get to the bottom of this."

Annoyed at the incessant interruption to his morning breakfast, Liam Bradly strutted toward the door. A continuous thunderous roar hammered his head, thanks to his addiction to good wine. He'd stupidly over-indulged at the wedding and his queasy stomach was a stark reminder of why he usually drank red instead of white wine.

He ran his hand through his hair and glanced at the wall clock. "Are you serious?" *It's not even* nine o'clock yet. Who the hell visits this early on a Saturday morning, especially after a late wedding reception the night before? He'd tear strips off whatever idiot was on the other side of the door.

Liam threw the oak door wide open. "Do you have any idea what time…" He froze mid-sentence, his eyes glued to the petite woman standing before him. He'd remember her anywhere. As if he'd forget a woman of her beauty. Her wavy red locks hung just below her shoulders, framing her face. This was much better than the semi-business look she'd worn yesterday at the wedding, hair pulled back in a tight bun. Now, she was the picture of a woman that would tantalise any man, including him.

She's beautiful.

A soft smile curved her lips, but her eyes told a different story. The drumming in his head shot his mind back to the present. He smiled. "Well, well, if it isn't the Cupcake Killer in person."

She gasped. "You read it too?"

He nodded. "I'm sure everyone in town's read it. Hard not to see it. It was plastered all over the front page."

Her glossy, sapphire-blue eyes widened. Thrusting her hands on her hips she said, "That article is utter nonsense. They had no right to print that without any evidence. My cupcakes were not the reason those people got sick."

"Really?" he asked folding his arms across his chest and giving her an uninterrupted view of his taut biceps and clenched abs.

Her jaw dropped to speak, but nothing came out. The only indication that she was still breathing was the warm, crimson blush that had worked its way from her neck to her cheeks.

"I...um... I wanted to...um..." She bit her bottom lip and paused mid-sentence as if her voice had suddenly vanished.

What the hell is with her eyes? Their constant flittering movement, combined with his throbbing head, was making him nauseous. It was as if she didn't know where to look.

He was standing there in only his pyjama bottoms with the door wide open for the whole neighbourhood to see. A rush of triumph surged through his system. *Nice to know my body can still affect a woman that way.*

He gestured toward his lack of attire. "My apologies, I wasn't expecting visitors," he said as he waved her inside. "Come in while I get something more appropriate on."

She shook her head. "I'm fine. I just wanted to speak to Beth, if she was around."

Liam turned and headed back inside. "Happy to chat after I get dressed. Close the door after you come in will you?"

He hurriedly dressed and walked into the kitchen, half expecting her not to be there. But there she was, standing in front of the sliding glass door framed by the morning glow of the sun. She looked naturally beautiful in a quiet, understated way.

He shoved his hands in his trouser pockets. "Don't tell me... you've decided to cook me breakfast. I'm not sure my stomach can handle one of your delicious cyanide cupcakes this morning."

She spun and stared straight through him. It unnerved him. Colour leached from her face, leaving her white as a sheet. Stepping back, she stumbled.

Liam let out a string of curses as he lunged for her before she face-planted on the kitchen tiles.

"I'm sorry. That was meant to be a joke. Obviously in poor taste," he said, still holding her elbow and refusing to let go until he was sure she had both feet planted firmly on the ground. Liam rubbed the elbow he'd grabbed, trying to alleviate any discomfort he may have caused by his firm grip.

"Yes, poor taste, indeed," she said huskily, easing her arm from his hold.

"It seems we were both rather busy at the wedding yesterday, and after your triumph in the bouquet toss, you disappeared. We never got the chance to formally meet." He held his hand out, eager for the introduction. "I'm Liam Bradly."

She looked at him in bewilderment, as if he were speaking gibberish, then stepped back and thrust her hand out in his direction, clearly determined to keep him at arms-length. "Charlotte McCorrson."

He smiled and shook her hand. "Nice to meet you, Charlotte." His hand pulsed under her warm touch. A soft smile curved her lips, her eyes glittering under the morning sun.

She withdrew her hand from his grip. "I didn't know you were staying here. I actually came over to see Beth. I wanted to reassure her my cakes were not the source of the poisoning and that article is utter garbage."

"Well, as you can see she's not here, or Lincoln for that matter. They left for their honeymoon in the early hours of this morning, but I'm sure they wouldn't believe it anyway."

"Oh," she said anxiously. "I thought they weren't leaving 'til Wednesday?"

"My surprise wedding gift," Liam said. It was the least he could do for his best friend.

"Are you house-sitting for them?" Her eyebrows went up in question.

House-sitting? The thought would have most certainly filled him with dread. That was before he met Charlotte. Now the idea had merit. *I have holidays due, and Lincoln did say to make myself at home before they left.* A week relaxing in this quiet town, getting to know the locals, one in particular, was definitely preferable to heading back to Perth to his mundane job of counting numbers on people's tax returns.

"Yes, I'll be house-sitting while they're on their honeymoon. Maybe you can show me around town while I'm here," he said flashing his cheekiest smile.

She gave him a peculiar look, apprehension entering her gaze. She shook her head. "I'm sorry, I can't. I have to get to the bottom of this poisoning before my entire business is ruined."

"Why would someone want to ruin your business?" he pried.

Annoyance washed over her expression. "As if I would know. It's not like we have enemies in town. I'm sure it's all a big misunderstanding."

He was up for an adventure. "Maybe we could make a deal. You show me around town and I'll help you solve the mystery of the cyanide bandit, what do you say?"

Charlotte froze, panic firing her eyes. She hastily moved past him and headed for the door. "I'm sorry, I can't. Enjoy your stay in Ashton Point."

Her rejection felt like a punch to the stomach. By the time he got his thoughts together, she was gone. "What the hell just happened?"

Printed in Australia
AUHW010516140619
313412AU00001B/4

9 780648 532521